ONE DAY

TALES FROM THE EDGE

A COLLECTION OF SHORT STORIES

COLLECTED BY

PATRICE CHAPLIN

SESHAT PRESS

First published in 2019 by Seshat Press

ISBN: 978-1-9163041-0-9

SESHAT PRESS
An imprint of Northern Bridge Productions
Charity No. 1077637
Enquiries: seshat@amberbridge.co.uk

Front cover illustration: *Soho* by Chris Chaplin

CONTENTS

INTRODUCTION

Northern Bridge Productions is a Charitable Trust that was set up over twenty years ago and uses creativity against addiction. Our work is based on using the addict's untapped creativity to replace substance craving. We have taken workshops and performances across the UK and Europe with considerable success. In 2004 we published *Clean Time* a collection of short stories and accounts by established as well as first-time writers, giving insight into the world of addiction.

Fifteen years later we have gathered this new collection of short stories, some by writers who have known active addiction or witnessed its tyranny, but mostly writers who welcomed the chance to produce a story in a market where short stories are on the wane. We decided *One Day* should focus on some aspect of safety or the reverse.

As a writer, I think a short story is a beautiful composition and I have been fortunate to contribute in the past to varied collections including the London Magazine and the BBC. I am glad to reflect that rich past with this enjoyable collection. Gratitude to my editor Alice Thomas Ellis (Duckworth) for her guidance which never dies.

Patrice Chaplin
London, 2019

PATRICE CHAPLIN

Mistress

Charles told me to get a cab for eight that evening. When he gave me the address was I surprised? He was inviting me to his house. Where was she? I did not particularly want to meet the partner in this seemingly humdrum but unbreakable marriage in which passion had long since died, anymore than she would want to meet me.

He had described her as a comfortable woman who had given up on her looks, her sexuality, she had even let her hair go grey which he loathed. Grey hair frightened him. It announced the start of an unwanted tenancy of a willing and deteriorating place where the landlord might turn out to be death. He'd had a few artfully applied blond streaks himself to make sure the men under him who so coveted his position received no false hope. They waited, obvious as hawks, for aging or sickness to end his reign so it wasn't vanity that painted out the grey but common sense.

We often ate at Lockets, a restaurant near the House of Commons, so he could stay close to a debate and its celebrated bell marked the beginning and progress of the parliamentary sitting.

Charles wore his power like his clothes, effortlessly. He was naturally elegant and had a certain charisma that imbued even the fabric of his clothes with life. He never talked down to anybody and in my case that meant not even bothering with politics. My talent lay elsewhere.

He was surprisingly kind, especially about his wife. Her devotion to their grandchildren was touching and another reason to stay with her. He admired her goodness and defended her celibacy. Not wanting the intimate side of marriage had been her choice many years before and he pronounced a number I found hard to believe. Thirty years. If he had said thirty-one or twenty-nine, I'd have believed him. But thirty sounded wrong in itself somehow. He said he would never hurt her and she knew nothing about me. I wasn't sure about that either.

'What does she think you do?' He was an attractive man with appetite.

'We never discuss it.'

He told me to get the cab driver to avoid Hyde Park Corner as a visiting dignitary was attending a royal function and some roads would be closed. On reflection he did not want me to stand on a street in the cold waiting for a cab so he'd send a car to pick me up at seven thirty. He always wanted to show that although he couldn't give me what I might want, he would take care of me in little ways.

Suddenly, I did not want to go into that house. 'Couldn't we just go to the usual place?'

'But you're always saying you're kept on the outside and not allowed into my life. Yet when you get the chance–'

'So your wife is away?'

'She's in Milan.'

'How long for?' People come back. Even from Milan.

'I've asked the cook to do something special for you. A Spanish dish.'

'You don't like Spanish food.'

'No, but you do.'

'You don't know anything about Spanish dishes.' I was beginning to wonder what I'd get.

'I don't have to. The cook's Spanish. My wife is away until the weekend. It's perfectly alright.' His voice, serene and measured, could persuade tougher opposition than mine.

I decided to wear the strapless dress he particularly liked with a casual jacket of wild silk, deceptively cut, and that was all. He liked it simple and elegant. At the last minute I climbed down off the skyscraper heels and chose a plainer pair more suitable for a homely dining room and fireside. I put my credit card, keys and lipstick in the jacket pocket and turned the collar up. Then, I realised I was actually going into his house, that oasis of warmth and belonging I could only imagine.

This must be a serious step forward in the affair. Was he considering something more permanent? I was suddenly happy.

He was waiting at the gate to welcome me, a large shaggy dog behind him, and taking my hand he led me up the path, into the hallway, and softly shut the door. How many times in my fantasies had he done this? The moment contained a dozen alternatives I had choreographed in my lonely bed. He would press me with the insatiable longing against the closed door. He would lead me to the fireside and his lowering my body onto the rug would be gentle. Afterwards, he would assure me the house would be mine and she would be long gone, preferring life in the countryside with the grandchildren.

He kicked the dog's squeaking toy to one side, I had not

expected the dog, and shouted downstairs to the cook. The guest would soon be challenging the authenticity of the paella. Holding my hand, he showed some of the house and I could see he wanted to share it with me. He was always a gracious companion and probably a marvellous host. The place was not as I had imagined, stuffed with art on the one hand and children's toys on the other. It was stylish and arranged by someone who knew how to bring out the best.

A single red rose in a tall crystal glass placed against a green wall had all the impact of a powerful painting. The green brought out the essence of the rose. The mirrors and lights created subdued uniformity that was calming and harmonious. We passed through a muted understated territory and arrived in the formal dining room.

'I thought we'd be better downstairs.' He led me to a cosy room beside the kitchen with the table laid for two. The family ate here when they weren't receiving guests. During the tour of the tranquil rooms I had tried to look at the family photographs but he had sped past those and I felt the real life of the house was behind the doors he hadn't opened.

Charles turned down the lights, raised his glass and welcomed me to his house. His eyes said he loved me.

A glass door led onto a patio, which was lit discreetly. The proper gardens were in the country where his wife spent most of her time. The cook was introduced as a native of Valencia and there followed a short discussion on the origin of paella. He was pleased to speak in Spanish and promised paella in Valencia was impeccable. To begin with a Catalan speciality, fresh asparagus and other vegetables cooked on a charcoal grill with olioli sauce.

'Mr Charles does not like the food all mixed up but he will eat paella in honour of you.'

Charles lit the candles and I wondered if I would spend the night. He described his sailing boat and how he had taken it single-handed up the coast of Norway. Was it the specially purchased wine, a little rough, that made him sound proud? He stopped suddenly and laughed.

'You think I'm a little tipsy but I'm optimistic. Isn't that good? I'm optimistic for us.' He raised his glass.

At that moment I was aware of a taxi pulling up in the street above. Probably a dozen had pulled up during the twenty minutes we'd been at the table. Then followed the unmistakable sound of spiky heels hurrying. Was that the sound of the front door closing? The dog barked, pleased. Charles looked up, all optimism gone. Undeniably, the spiky heels were coming down the stairs towards us. I did, foolishly hopeful, think that such shoes could belong to a daughter. He didn't have one unfortunately. There was no time to hide. We were vulnerable as two clay ducks in the fairground. I did think the shoes would not belong to a comfortable grandmother with grey hair and no interest in sex.

I looked at Charles. He would have the solution. They called him The Peacemaker. Of course he'd have an answer. When they could not sort it out in The House, they sent for him. When the global conflicts were beyond discussion they asked him to take over. He was born to unify the incompatible. Like a scientist in a laboratory he blended opposing substances until they fused, adding a special sweetness I thought was love.

The shoes clicked louder like some killing machine. I could smell the perfume, expensive and plenty of it, could hear the shiver of silk, the dry stir of sharp diamonds hanging from ears and wrists. Charles' face became resigned. He just wasn't there. He'd said goodbye to life and was facing a firing squad and the shoes reached the lowest level and came towards us. No, first there was a cruel pause and they might, at some luckier time, have taken another direction. But they wanted to be where we were. Our reprieve was over.

Two things happened. An elegant blond came energetically

into the room and Charles threw his napkin over the top of his head so it hung down like a curtain covering his face. This made him invisible. She looked at him, one scathing look, then turned up the lights, blew out the candles, poured herself a glass of wine. This was her territory.

'I like to see what we are eating.' She looked at the paella. 'What's that muck?'

I told her it was paella and introduced myself. Her brown eyes as she assessed me were not altogether unfriendly. She didn't like the wine either. I explained it was a Rioja from Spain.

Charles still sat with the napkin covering his face. This white cloth could have been some truce signal but she wasn't having any of that.

'What kind of mess is this?'

Did she mean the relationship, Charles and mine? The food? I qualified my being there by saying I was interested in political debate. She wasn't having any of that either and called for the cook. Charles continued to sit, face covered up like the subject of a painting by the surreal artist Magritte. It seriously challenged my respect for him. The cook rushed into the room expecting a calamity. When he said how surprised he was that she was back he spoke for all of us.

'What made you even think of cooking something like this?' She pushed the paella dish aside.

'It is a traditional speciality from my country, Madam.'

'Not in my house. Bring me something to eat. Food. And decent wine.' Then she sat opposite me and the diamonds and sapphires glinted malevolently. He'd bought all these. At least he'd paid for them. Her hair was gold, lustrous, courtesy of a top stylist. She was toned up, tanned and fiery. Where was this comfortable sexless grandmother with the greying hair he dreaded? When she stopped hating the paella she'd turn on me. Nothing was changed in my lover's attitude. The napkin hung motionless and didn't even move when he breathed, if he breathed. I decided I should start my departure.

I'd been through too much in my time to let this misfortune really get the better of me. I said how delighted I was to meet her. She cut through all that with, 'What do you see in this muddle?'

Did she mean the extra marital affair which had now become an uncomfortable triangle? She meant the paella. She forked it around and tasted a piece of squid. I realised it stopped her thinking about the actual diners at the table. I asked if she knew Spain. However rattled I became I must not mention Milan.

'Spain? I've hardly been there. Charlie and I always go to the Islands.'

Charlie! He was now 'Charlie'. I asked her if she'd just been out of London. Not smart but I had to say something.

'Charlie certainly thought I'd be out of London. I don't know who is more surprised I'm in London, he or my cook.'

She poured some of the decent wine and talked about Milan, its shops and style and I found I slipped easily into the role of respondent in this conversation. We shared certain tastes, not just her husband. I managed to look her in the eye and answer her questions, all the while thinking, don't trust life.

Of course, Charles didn't think like me. He hadn't had the same experience. I'm not playing with all the dots on my dice when I, a 'Have not', trust 'the Haves'.

The cook brought her a nicely fluffed up omelette and wholesome salad. I began to get the distinct impression she liked me or would have in different circumstances. We kept on talking, style, cinema, fitness clubs, and he stayed unmoving, the napkin showing no intake of breath. Was he no longer with us in every sense? She took absolutely no notice of 'Charlie' and whistled to the cook to serve coffee upstairs.

'Let's get out of here. At least you talk.' She gave him one look, just one and it was lucky he was still behind the napkin.

The look made my blood and his bank balance go cold. Charles, or was it Charlie, did not stir so I followed her upstairs and left my love and all that passion behind, cooling faster than the paella.

She had something brave about her and I knew she'd been through it. In her case expensive pain – it still hurt and she had found the answer by tightening the screws and becoming smaller and harder. She hated cowards, more than infidelity. She'd discovered that tonight.

'If you want to powder your face use the lavatory next to the bedroom. I'm sure you're familiar with that one. Or do you prefer the guest bathroom?' I stayed silent and still. 'Go ahead into the drawing room. You obviously know where that is.'

So, I told her I had never been in her house before tonight. I had, though, noticed its effective and tasteful decoration. She must have engaged a superb designer.

'No, I did it.' For the first time she seemed almost pleased.

In the unknown drawing room below the bedroom, no he had not shown me this, we sat, each on a pale silk sofa and drank coffee from Italy. She still tried to trap me into a too intimate knowledge of her property, then stopped wasting time and got out the fabrics from Milan. She described how she was designing a friend's London house and Charles – he was never Charlie – had crapped in his own nest and she would never forgive him.

Away in the corners of the room, now I dared look, were discreetly placed informal photographs of my lover with world leaders. Then she asked political questions which, if I was as I described myself, I should have been able to answer. She stared at my dress, all friendliness gone.

'How do you keep it up?'

How did I keep anything up? Especially this performance. It was time to go. She wouldn't hear of a taxi. She would take me.

'It will take ten minutes.'

'But I live in north London.'

'The way I drive it will still be ten minutes.' She click clacked to the door.

'What about Charles?'

'What about Charles!' She opened the door and the shoes spiked their way along the path and the gravel spat.

I was still at the door inside the house. The cook was beside me. 'Goodnight,' he said. And I was outside the house and the door closed softly behind me. This was how death feels.

She walked past the Rover. Would she stop at the Bentley? No, the charming car with the fifties number plates would be hers. I was curious to see what she identified with. She passed the Porsche and slowed down by a Range Rover, then shot across the road and opened the door of a red Mercedes sports car costing more than I'd seen in my lifetime.

Before I was properly in beside her the car purred off and her hands in the leather driving gloves meant business. The car was on automatic and so was I. It would take the privacy of my rented bedroom to fully experience and come to terms with the paella dinner fiasco. The Spanish would have a word for it. Yes, she drove fast, biting up the road, overtaking cars as though they were standing still. Was she going to kill us both? Was this her solution? I tried to calm her by praising her purchase of several off-white linens which when hung together would be brave and effective. I wanted to say, 'Look, I know nothing about politics.' But she knew that. She knew about me. They always knew. She almost approved of me because I was not without a certain courage but she disliked me because I had thought to take what was hers.

Her skill handling the car was exceptional and I could not take my eyes off the way the gloved hands touched, clutched, stroked, tightened, gripped the wheel with a certain intent. The hands in the gloves were lethal. She would squeeze my throat and strangle me as meticulously as she drove a car. The gloves would do a tough job and leave no evidence. We spun around Marble Arch and the leather gloves steamed with fury. What had brought her back from Milan so unexpectedly? Me! Although I had given a false address the car hissed to a stop outside my house.

'I was wrong,' she said. I could only wonder what would come next. 'I said ten minutes. I made it in nine.'

I thanked her and, terrified, I left the car. She waited while I walked shakily along the path on the low-heeled shoes with the classic cut suitable for homely visits to a lover. When she was satisfied I had undeniably reached the door, the car whooshed off, screeching around the corner.

Charles? You could be celibate for thirty years with a Charles. But you made love with a Charlie.

ANTHEA COURTENAY

The Taste of Ice Cream

But this was all wrong, thought Lois, as the ceiling tilted and circled above her, and then began to slide at an angle. This wasn't supposed to happen! She clenched her fists as whatever she was lying on also tilted, downwards, but she was safely strapped in, and now she could see the back of the ambulance man in front of her. 'She's coming to,' said a male voice.

Then there was the sound of an engine, then her eyes closed and opened again, and now it was the sky circling above her, small white clouds she noticed, and then she was on a trolley, noisy wheels on rubber flooring, and her eyes closed again, and now she was in a bed and her hand hurt where a fat needle had been jammed into it.

And each time she woke she thought, 'But this wasn't supposed to happen!'

Why on earth had she believed that woman? Perhaps it was her motherliness. 'You're going to be fine,' Betty had said, small plump hands fluttering over brightly coloured cards. 'The sun! Everything turning out right, lovely! You've nothing to worry about.'

It had only been a short reading, ten or fifteen minutes, at the local psychic fair. Lois had never visited a psychic in all her fifty years. She had gone in nervously, but wanting to believe, because the doctors had to be wrong.

After her last scan they had looked at her with serious, over-kind faces, and told her they were sorry the chemo hadn't worked as well as they'd hoped, and she could opt for more, but it might be more comfortable – they suggested in a roundabout way – to let nature take its course. No, they couldn't say how long, but they indicated tactfully that she should get her affairs in order. No more chemo – good, her hair had only just grown back. And her affairs hadn't had the chance to get out of order since the original scare. They asked about her next of kin, and introduced her to a nurse-counsellor she could talk to any time – perhaps she'd like to join a support group? No, she wouldn't.

She couldn't understand it, she'd been feeling perfectly well. There must be a mistake. And on impulse, she had gone into the town hall where the psychic fair was held, and had chosen to have a reading with Betty, 'Tarot Reading and Mediumship'. Perhaps this total stranger, with nothing to prove, would be straight with her.

'Ah, you've had a little health scare, I see. But you're on the mend.' That's what she'd said. Nothing about the awfulness of waking barely able to move, the excruciating headache, the struggle to dial 999 before she passed out.

'The best thing is not to worry too much, worry always makes things worse, doesn't it, dear?' Betty was perhaps in her sixties, with pink hair and a full bosom, her low-cut blouse unashamedly displaying a crinkled cleft. She was warm, kindly, she seemed to know Lois, and for those fifteen minutes Lois wanted to trust her.

'There's lots of love around you,' Betty told her. Well, she was wrong about that – chance would be a fine thing! Lois had a couple of good friends at work; they got together for the cinema and meals out, and remembered each other's birthdays with cake and a visit to the wine-bar. But love? Lois knew she was not a person who inspired love; she had not felt loved since the death of her parents, several years ago. Even so, when she heard the words she savoured them.

'You have a very happy future! Roses . . . there's something about roses. Do you like roses, dear?'

Lois did like roses.

'Maybe someone's going to give you some . . . Mmm, I can smell them. There's some other flowers too – and what lovely colours. You're going to be very happy. It's almost as if . . . oh, I can see golden light, beautiful! That's symbolic, dear, you're going towards the light. Do you know an Eve?'

'My mother's name was Eve.'

'Well, she's here, my love, she's very glad you came to see me today, because she wants to send you her love, and let you know that everything's going to be all right.'

The nurses were wonderfully kind. Were they trained to be especially nice to cancer patients? From newspaper reports of hospitals, as well as her visits to the cool-mannered consultant, she hadn't expected them to be so thoughtful, so considerate. They were concerned about her pain, constantly checking to make sure that she was comfortable.

But she was puzzled, and annoyed. Psychic Betty had promised her a wonderful future. But the tumour was back. Under the battering of chemicals it had made itself very small inside her brain, and now it had popped up again, exulting: 'You don't get rid of me that easily!' For half an hour Lois suffered a burning anger, with the tumour, with Betty, and with herself for believing Betty. But she was too tired to be angry for long. She relaxed and let the nurses look after her; she had not been cared for like this since she was a small child.

Mavis, one of her work colleagues, came to visit. She brought a bouquet of roses, a wonderful salmon-pink tingeing into orange. As she unwrapped them, their scent wafted over Lois, momentarily masking the ambient odours of chemicals and cooking.

'You don't often get roses with a really good scent,' Mavis said. 'I was ever so pleased to get these.'

'They're lovely. Thank you.'

'Janet's coming to see you on Thursday,' said Mavis. 'She sends her love.'

Next day a big card arrived, signed by everyone in the office, not just Mavis and Janet, and Lois made sure it was put where she could see it, all those names, sending their good wishes. All those people caring about her – she would never have expected that.

A chaplain arrived out of nowhere, offering to pray with her. 'I don't believe in God,' said Lois, and rolled over, turning her back on him.

Somehow she'd stopped worrying; perhaps it was the morphine. She lay back and accepted what was happening, and found she was enjoying being looked after. She slept a lot. She dreamed about her parents, and the holiday they'd been on at Broadstairs when she was ten, and she ran over the smooth wet sand in her bare feet, and turned cartwheels and then they went for ice cream and it was the most delicious ice cream she had ever tasted, she'd never been able to find ice cream that tasted like that again . . .

We were a happy family, she thought, a truly happy family,

you don't get many of those. We three were really close. Perhaps that was why she'd never needed anyone else. It had been a shock when her parents went, one after the other, quite quickly.

Janet came as promised, and didn't say much, but held Lois's hand, and that was fine, because Lois didn't really want to talk, and having her hand held was unexpectedly pleasant.

Sometimes she was in her bed on the ward, and sometimes she was somewhere else. Today she was in a garden of gloriously coloured and scented flowers, there were roses among them, and other flowers she didn't know, and their scent was wonderful, and on the far side she saw her mother, wearing the sun-hat she had worn at Broadstairs, smiling and waving, and beside her, her father, also beaming and waving. She wanted to cross the garden to greet them, but then someone started shaking her to give her some medicine.

'Happy,' she said to the nurse, who smiled at her, and squeezed her hand, and stroked the hair back from her brow, before offering her a spoonful of ice-cream to help the pill go down, feeding her like a baby. It was good ice cream, but it didn't have that perfect Broadstairs flavour.

She swallowed the pill and the ice cream and closed her eyes again. And she was back in the garden, and the sun was shining, and it was sunshine such as she had never seen, gold, touching everything in the garden with unimaginable luminosity, and her mother and father were still there, and their love was like a golden wave pouring over her, and as she floated towards them she saw the ice cream cone in her mother's outstretched hand and knew with total certainty that everything really was absolutely all right.

STEVEN KUPFER

Romanian Proverb

A man in a dark-coloured jacket with a hood was walking down the street. He was carrying a lemon in his left hand. My mother and I watched him through the bay window in the downstairs front room of the house we lived in then. She said she was reminded of an old Romanian proverb her mother had recited. The whole thing, the man, his jacket with the hood, the lemon and the fact that he was walking down the street as we watched, made her feel the proverb was being enacted before our eyes. I asked her what the proverb was. She had forgotten it. I was six or seven years old at the time and I did not pursue the matter.

But I did not forget the incident. Once, some thirty years later, I mentioned it at the end of a lesson to a class of fifteen year olds. I asked them to go away and see if they could devise a proverb or saying, which, though it would not be the proverb my grandmother, whom I never knew, had told my mother, it might have been. When I read over what my students had written and saw how completely they, all of them, had misunderstood me I felt ashamed I had so trivialised this moment from my childhood.

Over the years it has occasionally come to mind and I have regretted I did not ask more of my mother's memory.

And I wonder why that moment remains so clearly in my memory when so much else has been lost or become blurred. We, my mother and I, are looking out of the bay window in the front room of our house in C. It has just stopped raining and the sun has come out and the street outside and the houses opposite sparkle in the sudden brightness. The man of the forgotten proverb appears before us walking slowly from right to left. His jacket is dark-grey and bedraggled and wet. The hood is half off his head as though he has responded to the passing of the rain but does not yet trust the sunshine. He holds the lemon in front of him like a candle, clasping it by its base, and its unmistakable lemon form seems to rise from between his fingers and gleams golden in the sunshine. My mother's voice has taken on a dreamy tone as she remembers her mother's words and though, like me, she is staring out of the window at the man passing in the street in front of us, when I look at her it is if she were seeing something else as well, something much more distant which is invisible to me. When I look back to the street, of course the man is out of sight.

Though itself so clear the moment is set amongst uncertainties, half-remembered, half-forgotten. They say that remembering tarnishes what is remembered; that what is recalled is always only the last experience of remembering, the latest most blemished copy in the series, and never the original moment. I will not have it so. I feel there is something in this incident that has persisted and is the source of my revisiting it and of the strange feeling, a kind of thrill, both painful and pleasant – perhaps poignancy best captures it – which it engenders. I feel sure that even now after so many years have passed if I attend closely to the memory I will understand something of what has made it so unfailingly fascinating.

Thus it has the feel of morning early in a year, when it is no longer winter and is not yet quite spring. The feel of morning because the sun is bright upon the street outside while the room, from which we watch the man as he passes, is in shadow. The room faces east and so the sun must be poised above the roof of our house, though not very high in the sky, for our small front garden too is in shadow right up to and including its low brick wall. As for the youth of the year, sunshine has its seasonal feel and I can find March or April there in the sparkle and glow of the lemon.

I realise too that there is another newness about the lemon. Lemons were then still strange to my world. I had learned of them a year or so before, from my alphabet book; 'L is for lemon so yellow and bright', and there it had been, yellow and bright on the page but until recently only on the page. Among its many effects, the war, which was not long ended, had emptied my world of lemons, a small void to be sure, of which I was not even aware until they had so recently reappeared. Certainly I must have seen this fruit before the day of the Romanian proverb, but not often. And I have no memory now of those previous encounters. On that day, carried so ceremoniously before us as if it were a jewel, and golden and glowing in the sunshine, light sparking off the raindrops which still cling to it, it seemed entirely new and strange.

Yet my mother's words in the shadowy front room recalling my dead grandmother and the Romanian proverb which she could not remember but which seemed to be played out before us, clothed the sparkling newness of the lemon in something much older. It was as if it were a re-enactment of a long ago incident we neither of us had experienced, which had happened in another country. Not Romania. For I would not have known that there was such a place.

Indeed, that the proverb was Romanian would have meant nothing distinct to me, only adding to the aura of strangeness of the scene re-enacting it. I am now not even sure of the exact word, for, though I seem to hear my mother's voice speaking to me, strangely, I cannot now tell whether she spoke in English. We often did not, especially in those days when my mother was still quite new to England. I knew that she and my father had come from another country that was always spoken of as home, a home I did not know and had never been to. It was a home to which at that time they still believed we might return. They never spoke of home in English. I always listened intently, always aware I was falling short, and that I was failing to get any firm picture of the place they spoke of. I had come to feel that we were strangers in some way that could be remedied only by return to that distant home.

Of course, my mother and father did not return and I have long outgrown the sense that I am a stranger here. Or better, perhaps, the decades that have passed have buried that sense of being a stranger in a place that was not home. I correct myself because now it seems that something of that feeling survives in my memory of the morning when my mother was reminded of the Romanian proverb, as we watched the man bearing the lemon pass in front of the window.

I have never asked myself who the man was nor what he might have been doing. He remains unwaveringly in profile as he passes, his gaze fixed to his front as if he were very near his goal and, full of purpose, could see it before him. His pace is unhurried and unchanging. He is not only unaware of my mother and me in the shadowy front room from which we see him pass before us. He seems to be unaware of the street down which he is walking. Perhaps this impression comes from the fact that he is walking in the roadway and not on a pavement. No one ever did that. I was always being told to stay on the pavement, even though in those days after the war no one possessed a car and there was hardly ever any traffic on our street.

But there is more to his unawareness than this for it extends to the street itself. I realise now that just as in a theatre, actions and words can transmute the space of the stage, change it into a space in some distant time and place, so my mother's words and the man's ceremonious progress before us dislocate the street, defamiliarise it. Nothing changes, our garden wall, the sunshine on the wet street, the red brick and shining windows of the houses opposite are all the same as ever. And yet all is different, is no longer here, but has become momentarily somewhere else, a different space in another time. It is the space of the Romanian proverb. Told to my mother by her mother, its words forgotten, its message unknown, yet somehow played out before us, it also enacts our own sense of displacement, of what I have since learned to call exile.

Perhaps this is why it has remained with me over the many years since we witnessed it in our front room, my mother and I. She is long dead now also. But sadly that moment is fresher than any other memory I have of her. For it seems to me now that though the incident happened in time on a particular morning in spring in the 1940's, when I was a child and my mother still young, it is also outside that time.

No, that it not quite right. I feel the wrongness. I have been too quick. Reluctantly, indeed with some pain, I have to recognise there is a difference between my mother's role and mine. I have seen us both as audience to a piece of theatre that momentarily transformed the real outside the shadowy front room. But when

I remember my mother's dreamy voice as she spoke of the Romanian proverb, saying that it was what her mother had told her and that it was now played out before us, when I remember her look as I turned to her, how she herself seemed removed from the room, her gaze fixed on something remote and invisible to me – I realise she is part of the moment in a way in which I am not. Like the street outside she is distanced, defamiliarised, a stranger to me while still remaining herself.

It is as if though still so close beside me, our bodies almost touching, she is also far away from me. And I do not like it. I am afraid. And when I ask her what the proverb says my question is not designed to find out what its words are. I want to bring my mother back to me from wherever she has gone.

She answered that she had forgotten what the proverb said. I turned back to the window. The man with the lemon was out of sight. The incident was over. My mother and I were in our front room together as before, as so often again. But it seems to me now that something had changed, something that would not be restored.

JEFF WATERS

The Peel of a Satsuma

So, Mary's cat got sick on Christmas Day and by the evening the creature was so bad she needed to find a 24 hour vet. We knew it was the most inconvenient day of the year for Tiger Lily to get ill and I'm not sure the cat didn't know that too and just wanted to blow a hole in Christmas for the fun of it. 'Come with me' she said 'you're not doing anything' which was absolutely correct given that both of us were moody bastards who had elected to spend the yuletide isolating, acting out and power sulking, the three unwise moves for the newly sober at Christmas. I was six months clean and dry with periodically reoccurring hallucinations and Mary was a little bit less with full-tilt paranoia and co-dependency issues. We were a charming pair, obviously warmly welcomed and loved wherever we went. A typical day back then was rocky to say the least but this one Christmas night the I-Ching was utterly unhinged and we found ourselves spliced into a special piece of delirium that our biographers might describe as 'memorable' or 'outstandingly bad'. That is, if anyone other than me would be stupid enough to write anything about two cranks careering around Kentish Town in an empty Ford mk2 transit van with no reverse gear, looking for someone to put a cat down.

We could have been with our families watching *Die Hard* and trying to get loaded on egg-nog, crackling fires, cold turkey sandwiches, quality street and all that shit, Uncle Cyril in a paper hat or watching the kids break their new toys but Mary didn't have anything in common with kids on account of their inability to get a round in so instead we were illegally parked in Duncan Terrace waiting for an inconvenienced vet to turn up to his clinic and give Tiger Lily the long lie-in. Frankly, he could've done all of us. We were as fucked as the cat. I was rocking with the anxiety, a chilling precision of dark ideas coming thick and fast, half in and half out of myself like an alien abduction survivor scanning the skies for any more weird lights and Mary, well she was on the sharp end of another all-consuming, three month sexual obsession with a beautiful blonde body-builder who had totally forgotten her an hour after they met. Naturally he came up in conversation. She wanted to know if I knew anyone with a gun and funnily enough, as it happened at the time I did but I said I didn't because things like that have a tendency to escalate somewhat. She wanted to go round and shoot the body-builder for not returning the love and no amount of nonsense from me about 'free choice' or 'personal rights' were going to change the fact that he deserved to die for making her feel this way whilst being so 'hot' at the same time. We'd been here before sadly. She had a real propensity for obsessing on entirely inappropriate and unavailable men, who were way out of her or anyone else's' league and who would only have caused her piteous misery anyway. Her relationships were torture and I advised her to do what I do and rough it with any piece of shit who returned the favour. We agreed it might be a good idea to go to an AA meeting or something.

By now Tiger Lily had 'transitioned peacefully to the non-material' and after a bit of sobbing and shitting on about how 'special' this cat was to her (pure lies – loathsome, empty-headed creature that destroyed everything with urine and went missing until it wanted something) we watched while the sleepy Vet bagged up the corpse and took a card payment. Double-bubble for Christmas, of course. Carols at King's College was on in the background and impossibly fresh-faced pre-pubescent boys exchanged earnest glances in the candlelight, making 'O' shapes with their innocent mouths while Mary and I watched in abject contempt, as irredeemable as two of Satan's imps by comparison. Our appearance was alarming. Something like a pair of rejects from a street-drunk's enactment of the musical 'Hair' perhaps. She had these sunglasses with lenses that were white plastic stars and an unruly Afro that stood at least a foot off her head while I resembled a 70's Scandinavian pornographer with a peroxide crop and handle-bar moustache and that louche availability that's always so attractive on an ex-pisshead. Frankly, looking back I can see why the vet was nervous. Fuck him. We made everyone nervous. People would pay a stylist a lot of money to look this shit and we were both far too self-obsessed to worry about image anyway. I was just glad I wasn't hearing things in the pipes anymore and Mary never set much store on trying to impress people. In fact, she'd target you. I once watched her upbraid a billionaire for not being grateful enough for his good fortune when everyone else was trying to kiss his arse. 'There's a Slags Anonymous meeting on round the corner,' she pronounced with a sudden and unnerving certainty, referring to the sex and love addicts 12 step meeting in Duncan Terrace. Given the acute nature of her latest romantic disappointment I considered it prudent to help get her in there before she drove a white builder's van into this bloke's front garden. Also we were bored now we'd killed the cat.

Shiny faces, not at all desperate looking, Hello, hello, nice to see you, tea, cheers, happy Christmas . . . how many times have you thought about raping someone today? Straight in there. I sat with eye-raising equanimity as the dozen or so people in the room exchanged sex-addict small talk about getting on packed tubes. One open heart from Dalston Kingsland told us of his sadness at not being allowed in the fruit aisle of Tesco's anymore and a Lithuanian exchange student bemoaned the injustice of being served an ASBO for painting a face on her arse in make-up and showing it to passing traffic on the Euston road. Is this Mother Russia! I drank enough tea to drown a vicar and anxiously scanned my past experiences for something beefy or sleazy enough to hold its own in such rarefied company. Jarringly, Mary starts up. A long and baroque monologue of betrayal and rage aimed sometimes at the erstwhile fella, other times at the general unloving faces of her past. We all nodded and concurred. Yes, people are shits and none of us were loved enough. Jaffa cake? After ten minutes of this I started giving her the 'wrap it up' face but she steam-rollered on and resentful fidgeting became contagious.

'Thanks, Mary . . . ' says the Secretary in a good-natured attempt to shut her the fuck up but Mary was in full sail now, HMS Mary, eyes rolling in the sockets, a sort of deranged puppet of bitterness and acrimony, her arguments for castration and manslaughter about as reasoned as Charlie Manson's cookery tips.

'I don't think this is healthy,' interrupts one, 'I'm offended by that' says another. I thought, this can't go on, and thankfully the universe agreed and Mary was officially asked to relinquish sharing to someone else in the room, until it was politely suggested we fuck off. 'This is Slags Anonymous isn't it?! You can say anything, can't yer?' her Leeds burr always at the front when she was properly pissed off. Lots of people talking, cross-sharing. Cups rattling and odds on whether I'd meet any of these people again or be recognised by them in court running through my mind like risk assessment. Finally she leaps up, calls them all cunts and says 'come on Jeff' at which I follow, apologizing, like a Mandarin's servant. It's not often you get thrown out of Slags Anonymous.

Outside, the Christmas night was clear and iron cold but it was a relief to be free of that room with its 24 giant, perverted eyes, 28 if you included us two giant perverts. The stars were abundant but bore down on me with all the weight of eternal irrelevance they could summon. No answers out there, sunshine. We climbed into the white transit van which was colder than Dante's ex-wife and we watched our breath pull in and out as we waited for the adrenalin to dissipate. This was now 'Outsider Art' and new for me to be forcibly ejected from a 12 Step meeting. This shit normally happened in the pubs! Traditionally I was safe and agreeable in meetings, any sort, AA, NA, SA . . . I did them all, but shackled to the Medea of Moorside I didn't stand a chance. Clearly, events were arranging themselves against us but the engine turned over with a grim fatalism as she announced, 'let's go kick his door in'.

We did meet up again, years later when we lived in Liverpool. Both her kidneys had collapsed while watching Eastenders one day at home and when they rushed her into the Royal they told her she had blood cancer as well so not only were transplants not an option but she couldn't have dialysis either with active cancer. 'I'm fucked, mate' she reliably informed me. It was Christmas again. We rowed like never before about 'leaving' each other again and out of petulant savagery on my part I ignored her for two months. When I saw her again she was unable to speak, had bloated to twice her size and was halfway to becoming an inanimate object. One of the last things I did was to feed her a rather sour Satsuma, which in its self was a bitter irony because she hated Satsuma's. She grimaced, all she could manage, and I saw that even with the shadow of destiny lowering implacably over everything there was still a little glinting shard of her humour. People didn't really like Mary but she was my friend and I loved her. She would tell me about being a kid of 8 or 9 in Leeds and looking out at the rain on a Sunday being furiously, desperately, destructively bored. I knew that feeling. I didn't fancy Mary's chances but at least I understood her odds. The earth is flat and the edge is like a sea shore. Things take you out and bring you back, each event pushing the limits but returning you to dry land, until one day the real edge appears and you're gone forever leaving only a few footprints on the shore, some crazy stories or the peel of a Satsuma, perhaps.

DAISY FINER

A Tale From the Edge: No Ordinary Death

Sometimes the body hears the news before the brain. The sound of the headline shoots down your limbs. A cascade of champagne coursing through blood. Bouncing against the rigidity of bone. As the language hits the limbic, as the words sink in, it feels like something has invaded the solar system of your internal universe. What is this, you wonder, enjoying the thrill of the rocket into space, a heightened rush, like the discovery of drugs. You know that something is happening. The delivery of a message from above. Remember this moment, it says on the envelope. Mark it out. Nothing will ever be the same again. Absolutely everything will change. From this one moment, on this one day, your life will be divided; there will be before, and there will be after (N.b., you're not enjoying this anymore). The 'Before IT Happened', that will feel safe, even though sometimes it was often hard. Blood, sweat, tears. Love tested to the extreme. But it will still feel like home compared to what came next. His name was Suicide, but we called him Smudge. We thought he belonged to us, but then he took his own life. (You're on your knees now, surrendered supplication).

They say the blood runs cold, that you feel it to your bones. But I didn't recognise it; it was new, this body language, to me. Against the natural order of things. I heard it say: my brother is dead. The brain told me, over and over again. He is dead. dead. dead. Disbelief cried out – NO. Just in another room, about to walk on in, wink, smile at me, hold my hand, call me Sis. To be, or not – that surely *is* the question. And when we did be-lieve, precisely then, that is when we fell. Meteorites shooting through the abyss. The world in freefall. You could say, the sky came down. The pins dropped out. We shook. We shake. Take off the mask. An individual revolution. That is what he gave us, that is what he lived. And nobody wants to mention the 'S' word. No one likes to talk about it. But everybody close becomes the detective. He died whilst on our watch, you see.

It wasn't just me. There were four of us. A maiden and three knights. Smudge was our elder, we looked up to him, we thought he knew everything, that he knew best. Only, it's not about knowing: his knowing, our knowing or knowing someone else. Blood of our blood, our very own DNA. Which would explain the impending sense of doom, honestly you could touch it in its potency – that force of destiny. That's where the guilt comes stabbing in, the endless backlash suffering of not having saved a life. ('My name is Daisy Finer and even though I knew he was going to do it I did nothing to stop my brother from killing himself').

During the period of his fragmentation, which took about six years and occurred between the ages of 18 and 23 (detective hat on) – when he finally became lost to us – Smudge had no idea what was happening to him, what was wrong. He even had a brain scan, to see if he was scarred on the inside, which of course he was, but the scan did nothing to explain his behaviour. The diagnosis was grandiose: psychotic schizophrenic. He was hearing voices in his head; learning to manifest in spectacular style an intense, underlying, visceral anger. The monster born inside. A hatred of mankind. They call it 'bottling up', and yes, he buried it deep. Put it in a box, Pandora's – pretend it never happened. That wasn't a choice, I don't think. Sometimes, when bad things happen to us, we don't want to face the demons, or give Satan the privilege of his name. It's safer to stay silent. Smudge never mentioned sexual abuse (uncomfortable isn't it).

The thing is, we didn't know the teachers were at play. My mother had no idea. My father neither, though it was my mother I later felt betrayed by. How could she not have known? But that wasn't until years later. It all happened a long, long time ago now, before paedophilia got such a bad name. From the age of 6 to 13. Right when Smudge was just becoming. The teachers in this boarding school, they slept in the dormitories with the children. That would never happen now. When the police got involved, around the time Smudge must have decided he'd do anything not to stand in court, the whole school was closed down. No other fruit more forbidden. No other pursuit so well hidden. For the Lord said you may not eat from this forbidden tree. Warm offspring of the womb. Juicy pomegranate of the underworld. The agony of the ecstasy. No wonder he really wasn't coping. 'Out of his mind', they called it. He had become unrecognisable as the person we knew. So, it's not like we weren't expecting it. This was no bolt from the blue. It terrified us, the three of us, his siblings, and what we knew. Though I guess the noose around the neck was a bit of a clue. Apparently, everyone tries in advance of the final act. It's rarely a curtain call at the beginning.

In the end he didn't hang himself. Though it shouldn't really matter. He went home, flew to the nest. He had supper with my parents. I don't know what they ate, but he loved mushroom soup and pasta. By this point the emotion was an ocean. He was occupying a different dimension. Every day a battlefield. My father said to him that night, 'you give us so much grief it's like your dead'. How could he have known? How would you? That the grief when you lose someone to suicide, it is like no other. A slow, insidious, distasteful shadow. It haunts you forever. The loss itself, the same as any other. The message he is gone. But suicide, arghh the grief, it is so different. Bless me father for I have sinned. Committed. You commit it. Sin of all sins. Drive to the garage, buy some petrol. Return to the Georgian Rectory. Sit down on a sofa. Drink a bottle of Jack Daniels. Watch Platoon. Call some pals for a little bit of chit chat. Mostly girls. But don't say much. His psychiatrist wrote on those scanty, inadequate notes of his, 'has problems with intimacy'. But that was as far as the psychiatrist got. On the day, the one day, the day life changed forever, my mother called this psychiatrist and told him, 'I'm really worried about Alexander' (Smudge was just our nickname and not for the professionals). When the psychiatrist rang back the next day, the wrong day, not the one day, my mother just said, 'you're too late, he is dead'. Dead: it goes around inside your head.

We are the forgotten mourners. When you lose a spouse, you are a widow. When you lose your parents, you are an orphan. There is no word to label someone who has lost a sibling, or a child. Nothing written spells it out. Other than the word, 'survivor'. Surviving, that is where the rest of us are at. Still now. Twenty years on. This family of mine. Live the shattering of the egg over and over again, knowing that there is only one life you can save. The weight, it gets no lighter. Your spine just gets stronger, stricter at carrying it. You are a zebra amongst the horses, dressed up as one of them. I like to think Smudge is merely waiting for us in a distant land. And I like to know that it is a power like no other to look Lucifer in the eye, turn away and continue to build a ladder to the stars.

He walked into a field. It was England, beautiful and in bloom. The month of May. Blue skies, as blue as his eyes, lilac blossom, the beginning of winter's wake. But what we see externally is by no means a reflection of our inner world. Suicides often happen in spring. No hope, it sets in. He poured the petrol over himself. Yes, I'm afraid so. He set fire to himself. My brother, he burnt himself to death. Not on the oven, but on purpose. It must have hurt like Hades. His body on fire in alignment with his soul. He was flown to a specialist burns unit. By helicopter. He would have liked that. When I got there, my parents were clinging to each other. He had 98 degree burns all over his body. If he had lived, he would have no hands. 'I'm dead, aren't I?' he said. I hate that he knew that. It makes me cry. My father kissed him goodbye on the soles of his feet because it was the only part of his body unmarked. When they turned the life support machine off it took him four hours to die. It felt like a long wait.

MALCOLM BRUCE

The Sins of the Father

After a short wait the healer ushered him into the treatment room. She asked if he would remove his shoes and lie down on the table.

'Now, I'm just going to tune in to your energy field for a couple of minutes. No need for you to do anything, just relax.'

She placed her hands above his body, one approximately above his solar plexus, the other above his forehead. An image began to emerge in her mind as she swooped down like a bird in flight flying through the peaks and valleys that are the scenes and interludes of his life, past, present and future.

'This is interesting,' she began. 'I'm not sure that I have seen this before. It's as if you had already transcended the cycles of your karma and did not need to be reborn into human form, but that you chose to come back as you still have something to do.

Something your spirit still wants to achieve on this plane.'

She began to swirl her hands and direct a healing force into the different energy centres in his body, supporting her physical movements with certain sacred sounds creating a powerful resonance that seemed to enliven his awareness.

'Your life experiences this time around have dampened your awareness. You must work on releasing the traumas and come back to a sense of your true essence. You certainly are a survivor, you've been through it. Perhaps that's what the journey is about for you, to overcome and transcend the challenges, and be a beacon of light for others. Now there's a life purpose that is worthy.'

As she continued her physical motions accompanied by the strange otherworldly sounds, a rush of memories began to emerge in his mind. All these experiences and feelings that had somehow become embedded and repressed, forgotten histories never fully processed and released.

Suddenly, he remembered a time as a teenager when his father, a world-renowned musician regarded as one of the great innovators of his time, asked him if he would perform at a special event for a prestigious music school in West London. They would perform in a trio alongside a drummer in front of 300 bass students. He was enthused by the opportunity. The day came for the performance and as they installed themselves backstage at the school, his father started to drink. After the second or third bottle of wine (and who knows what else), the 3 musicians entered the arena. Hundreds of students, armed with notepads and pens, looked down on them in the round as if they were godlike gladiators about to spar with each other in a great battle of sonic delight. They had obviously been prepped for the occasion and understood that having someone of this calibre performing for them was deemed as something quite special.

Eight and a half bars into the first song, and his father stops.

Moments later with seeming obliviousness to his surroundings he lurches into another number. He glances at the drummer whose gills are starting to look a little grey. The drummer glances back, attempting a faint smile that flickers across his already simultaneously tightening and sagging demeanour. Moments later, it happens again. His father transitions with indiscriminate superciliousness into another song. The musicians are collectively starting to sweat. He looks up at the audience who are emitting a deathly quiet anticipation whilst holding their breath in a unity that is most definitely not obvious between them in the pit.

Needless to say, the feted performance didn't last long. With some strange embarrassed only half admitted excuses between the musicians and the officiates backstage, devoid of any real sense of limpidity, they were limping backwards out the door.

He walked slowly and methodically in silence with his father to his car and they drove off into the glare of the afternoon sun that should have been glorious rather than oppressive. It was as if the sunlight was magnifying and confirming the cold realisation of what had just transpired rather than warming their hearts and consolidating their victory. They hit the motorway heading towards his father's house. His father was mumbling, despondent, aggressive, in a bubble of quiet anger, revving the engine, increasing the speed. Approaching 120mph, he holds on to the edge of his seat sensing the increasing tightness mounting in his body. His father begins to turn the wheel leftwards and glides closer to the edge of the road, closer and closer to the barrier, as if he wants to tempt both their fates by seeing how close he can get without actually touching. Maybe even go all the way and do them both in. Who knows? Finally, at an exit his father pulls over and drops him off at the side of the road, and without a word speeds off into the late afternoon abyss, leaving a cloud of dust in his wake. There he stood, guitar in hand, thinking to himself that he had been lucky to get out of that one alive.

He was reminded over the years of that day when he started meeting bass players who had been there. He realised that what could have been a fruitful experience at the beginning of his career had left an enduring and negative impression on him, and that he had somehow buried the memory beneath his awareness along with all the other unmanageable experiences. What could have been a nurturing and bonding time between father and son was in fact fairly traumatic and needed to be hidden. And of course it was his stepmother, not his father, who had apologised, on his father's behalf, which became somewhat of a pattern in their relationship. Things left unsaid, excommunicated. He was sure that if they could have blamed him for it they would, never taking responsibility and passing the buck being part of the same pattern. The normalisation of that kind of dysfunction was to become established and frequented throughout the years. The legitimately great artist playing the game with himself of being the illegitimately 'tortured artiste' and damn the consequences. A tensile layer that his father only very late in life was able to look at and perhaps address, and only in death was he to fully release from those destructive patterns. And the repercussions of those behaviours on his familial relationships were still unfolding, still affecting.

'Look, it's not going to be easy,' the healer continued. 'Others will resist you and even attempt to undermine you because the divine will beckon them to return via the light shining through you as a reflection of themselves, and they might not be ready. That resistance and its realisation and release is what it's all about in the incarnate journey. Does that make sense?'

He thought about it for a moment. He could see how all the

issues in his life might be construed as an enticement to return, to release, to learn to be 'in the moment'. And in that moment his breath softened, and he realised how the sense of physical restriction was inextricably linked to that resistance in the mind.

The healer recognised his thought process. 'Yes, you can see it now. None of this really exists in the way we can end up seeing it. If release happens, more and more we see that all is divine love, divine light. We see that fear is simply the result of having the blinders on, manifest as muscular contraction, the holding of the breath. It's the incorporeal versus the corporeal. It's all just concepts, perceptions open to interpretation, but these are things we inevitably need to utilise in order to understand the mundane when we find ourselves in this manifest form. But we forget how these are just representations. The divine is way beyond all that tiny nonsense.'

He saw that all of his Stygian nightmares *were* simply an invitation. And that all the human systems of understanding paled in comparison to divine intuition. That the thinking forms were burnt away in the brilliant light of truth. One stops thinking, and thought happens.

Thanking the receptionist as he paid for the session, he walked down the three flights of stairs to the exit and stepped outside onto the pavement. The mid afternoon sunlight immediately enveloped him in a warm loving embrace. He felt born anew. His breath was effortless and all was exactly as it should be. He saw that all was love and that he could leave the rest behind. The flood gates had opened and the insight began to flow, not through some kind of effortful thought process but from a vital intuitive force. He noted that absence of effort, of agenda, there was no separation. The awareness simultaneously contained all the characteristics he had come to know as who he was and at the same time was united with every speck of creation and liberated from fear. And that sweet spot of effortlessness seemed to allow all the constructs and patterns to be recognised for what they are; sometimes useful and required, but ultimately relative, addicting and consuming. Everything that had appeared as so important to maintain was realised in that moment as superfluous and ephemeral in the wake of this infinitely widening space.

And he finally understood: what appears here is simply a trigger for emancipation from illusion and that beckoning is ever present. There is alignment with only what is seen. We are blinded by the dark not the light. The light infuses with grace and strength and true power. All the transient dark forces cannot withstand the eternal omnipresent light. There is no competition between them. It is just a game played by the light. The dark shadows only appear when an object eclipses perspective. If the object is large enough then it can be momentarily mistaken for all that is there. But an object can never devour or contain the light, the light is all encompassing. Therefore any restriction is a pretender and never the ultimate victor. In this way we are already that which we seek. We only have to remove the objects precluding our vision. There is nothing we therefore have to learn. We simply remove restriction by going into stillness, not by doing that, but by releasing the forceful foot that constantly pushes down on the throttle of action. The eclipsing objects of illusion dissipate and the light rushes back in to infuse our consciousness. We are undone, born again into liberation and the eternal song of the divine once again is sung through us and all around us. Nothing, No Thing, matters.

The sins of the father, or the illusion of karma, re-cognised, by no-one. Blame, responsibility and even forgiveness an arrogance, an imposition, a ruse. All is as it is, all is appropriate in that sacred balance, not through affectation or addition or growth or learning or letting go, but through immediate grace. All falls away, action happens of its own accord, and it is understood that there is no separation between the objects in perception and the self. The self is an idea, the self is also an object arising in awareness. All is subjective and there is no-one here. The divine is simply experiencing itself through manifest form. The journey never happened, it only appeared as such as an enticement to return. Beginnings and endings are seen as mere concepts, abstractions with no intrinsic meaning. All that is left is divine, radiant and infinitely blissful light.

SHANTI MAYI

'He' is My Heart

There I sat in the midday shade, drinking a cup of chai, watching the current of the Ganga and feeling an anticipation that I had not felt before in my life. I was trying hard to be patient until 4:00. I was told that I could meet Maharajji at 4:00. And now I was waiting. I had arrived in Rishikesh a couple of weeks ago. After two years, I felt that I had returned to my heart's home. I missed this place . . . The scene filled my eyes. I felt fortunate and grateful. I was happy to be back. I was about to meet Maharajji. I didn't know anything about him, I only knew that Subash, an Indian cloth merchant I knew from before, told me I should come here. When he told me of a Saint that lived in an ashram in Laxmanjhula, I started out immediately in that direction. My feet flew so swift, as though I was racing toward a finish line. For three miles and up a long hill, along the winding Ganga, I flew. Attracted to what, by what? I didn't know. When I came to the gate of the Saint's ashram, a little old South Indian lady snapped at me that Maharajji wasn't available (in Hindi). Although I knew no Hindi, I knew exactly what she said. I stood there and waited anyhow. She looked at me as though I was crazy and left. I stood there waiting. Finally an older Swami came by, he told me to return at 4:00. Maharajji would see me then. So, now here I am; waiting. My heart pounding with anticipation. OK enough is enough, it is 3:45, I'll go. Arriving again at the gate of the ashram, the same Swami took me to meet Maharajji. There on his veranda he sat with a few people around him. I looked at him and my heart fell to earth. It was as though the light in my heart melted into a pool at his feet. There it stayed, it was his. My God, I met him only a minute ago, and already he had taken my heart forever. I looked deep into his eyes and raised my face eye to eye with his. Filled with an overwhelming humility, these words, 'I want to be just like you' passed my lips. Looking at me as though I was not really there, yet straight into the depths of my being, he said 'You will be.' I knew then that I would never leave him. I never have left him, not even for a second. There were Swamis sitting with him. They nudged each other with their elbows mocking me. 'She wants to be just like him' ha, ha. I knew they didn't understand, and I knew it didn't really matter. I too didn't understand. It was just the moment, just the throbbing of my heart and in that very moment, my life was handed over to him beyond my own will. I was relieved and grateful at once. It was in a flash that I knew I would live more by trust in him, than by air or food. He told me, 'I could feel your approach coming up the hill today.' I was touched by his recognition of me, for surely I had recognized him.

I went to my room that evening filled to the brim with our meeting and now I was different than I had ever been in my life. I cannot say what the difference was. One thing I knew, for sure, I knew that I had found my Master. As I settled in, I began to write him a letter and asked him to pierce the knots in my heart. I didn't know I had knots in my heart, but yes I did and the wisdom that he is, would loosen the knots and his grace would release me from the bonds of my ego. I woke up early the next morning and by 5:00 AM I again flew on winged feet to Laxmanjhula. In the ashram I waited for him to come out of his room and sit in the morning sun. I waited until 10:00 AM. From the day that I met him, I was always with him no matter where we were. If he was in his room he was with me. If I was in the town, he was with me. When he came to the veranda, I gave him the note. He read it and said that the night before, inwardly he and his Guru sanctioned my discipleship. My days were filled by sitting next to him in silence. Our silence went so deep that hours dissolved into minutes and minutes dissolved into eternity. In silence together we dissolved. Life and its content gone. There for hours, drenched in the silent teachings. Then, all of a sudden, in the twinkling of an 'I', the eternal appeared as the finite and life surrounded us again. There were times our silence was so powerful that only grace could pierce it.

As years passed between us, he taught me that the nature of existence is God. That God is all there is. Where nothing is, universes lay dormant, still and unformed by thought. Everything is emptiness, essentially. Emptiness is silence, memory and potential. He was teaching me inwardly. No one took notice. I thought that this was very good. Still, everyone could see the profound surrender I had for him and the love that we had for our time together. This time was indeed precious. He was forming me and I was helpless and thankful that my life had taken this turn. Now I would live for the rest of my days surrendered to him. As the seasons rolled one into another I realized that Maharajji, was a true Master of surrender.

It was by surrender that his Guru, Sacha Baba Kulanandji entered him completely and trusted him to carry his work forward. It was Maharajji's unwavering love and devotion to his Guru and Baba's grace that matured him into a Siddha Guru. Maharajji didn't speak to me of his past very much. Sometimes he spoke of the greatness of his Master and the love he had for the Baba. He told of the grace that was shed into his life. That grace is like a constant lamp that lights his way even today. In many different ways I was told about Maharajji's awakening.

Maharajji was always slight in his body, like a willow. He had a stomach disorder most of his life. It is told that he became so chronic in his stomach that he was ready to give up his life. At that time he was a bookkeeper by profession, with a wife and three children. A fellow worker asked Maharajji to visit his Guru in Allahabad, known as Sacha Baba (True Father or Mahatma of the Absolute Truth). Maharajji didn't see much use in it, but agreed. He made one condition and that was that he would not pay the Master even the simple honour of a bow, unless he fixed his stomach. In one account of this story, it is said that Maharajji also stated that if the Mahatma, Sacha Baba did not heal him, that his next alternative was to sink himself in the Ganga and leave the matter to God. I would like to inject here that this is what is told to me after collecting the story through so many people. I can imagine Maharajji's intensity. Though he is very mild and infinitely loving, he does have a side to him that is like a roaring lion. It is also quite natural for him, yet that side of him is rarely seen. So as the story goes, Maharajji agreed to meet Baba. Upon first sight of the Baba, our Maharajji fell at the Baba's feet. And in the same moment realized his true nature. It was such an overwhelming experience for Maharajji. After all, he came for a healing not for awakening. Baba ordered him to rest and he did for a long time. Then Baba came to him and told him 'You are Hans Raj, the king of the true Self.' From there, the years with his Master began. His stomach never got better, as a matter of fact to this day it is his major physical weakness. Still, he found his total strength and power in his Master's grace. It was Maharajji's determination and resolve to fulfil his Master's wish. It was by his absolute surrender to Baba that his life has been dedicated to the awakening of all beings. He never questioned the surrender to his Master's wish, he just went forward and has given his every breath ceaselessly to Baba. Baba said he must live for the awakening of the entire universe (not just this world). Baba used to say, 'All are my hands and all are my feet. All are my ears and eyes, but Hans Raj, you are my heart.'

As I sat outside his door day after day, his prayer for humanity poured grace over me. Each day, I could see even more clearly what his Guru wanted from him. He sat by himself in silence communicating in an incomprehensible way to the deepest receptivity in consciousness, that all beings must awaken. He has given his life to it and he has asked the same of me. Each day, his day is still filled with the command of his Master and each day is filled with our Maharajji's way of serving existence.

And so it was in 1988 as I sat with him in silence he looked at me with the flashing eyes and said 'Some day you will wear my shoes.' I didn't know what it meant so I tucked it into my heart and left it as a secret to blossom as it may. The Guru's word always bears fruit at one time or another. It always bears fruit. In the warm Indian afternoons, I felt so grateful to sit next to him as he slept on the veranda. He, behind the grass screen and I on the other side. I could hear an occasional snore, the sound curled up like a child at rest in my heart. There were very powerful times and very sweet times. There were times of stark learning and detachment. Though mostly we sat in silence. The silence was my refuge. There, it was tender and empty at once. It was in silence that he gave me the most profound teaching. Even the love and admiration for who he is, melted into the stillness. Once in a while he would cast a verbal gem into the pool of my heart. When he spoke, I listened. Even the sound of his voice was enough. I did not even need to understand what he said. In the evening he would come out and sit with us. It was always a very special time. This evening would be like all others in some way and different as well. Together we sat under the mango tree, just him and me. He bent over very directly, looking me straight in the eyes and said 'There is not a particle of reality in any of this.' We knew the oneness and the emptiness and the play of consciousness within our 'Self.' Like two birds we sat quietly, unmoved by the people slowly gathering around him. Everyone adorned in the twilight of evening and the Master's grace. The moon rose above the mango tree. The soft glow of light defined the meditative faces of the people. The lila played out as a moonlit evening with the Master. I played my part in silent observation.

CHARLOTTE TRENCH

A Box of Bones

The coffin felt surprisingly light, almost floating on Clara's fingertips. It was made of cardboard. And her stepmother must have been skin and bone by the end. The pallbearers in front, Eliza's two granddaughters, were taller than Clara and the men bringing up the rear were both big. So the oblong brown box didn't sit on Clara's shoulder or on Neil's, the nephew walking beside her. They both made like they were supporting it with their hands.

After perfectly planned hymns and prayers in the chapel, close family only were driven to the crematorium, behind the long black car. When the little bunch met up on the steps a quiver of apprehension crossed Clara's half-sister's weary face; one of the pallbearers was missing. Not being a relation, he hadn't considered himself a close family member. Unexpectedly,

Clara found herself stepping forward to replace him.

Aligned with the other five, she inched her way cautiously towards what must be the crematorium oven, behind flowers and thick greyish-green curtains. Never in her wildest dreams would she have imagined herself carrying Eliza's coffin.

High heels and silky nylon stockings, a tight skirt. Her first vision of her stepmother was in the Ladies at a fancy tea-room. Clara's tummy felt funny, she'd never been taken out for tea before, sticky cakes with a thick layer of cream and a cherry on top that you ate with a fork.

Eliza loomed over Clara who was huddled on the loo with her feet dangling down.

'Are you alright?'

'Yes.'

Clara looked up. Eliza had red lipstick on. She backed out and the door closed behind her.

Later on at the circus Clara was sitting next to her father. Glittering beams slashed the blackness enfolding them. A brown bear cavorted in the middle of the pale ring far below. Clara was intensely aware of the warm bulk of her father as he leaned forward, his daughter forgotten, focusing on the animal.

A roll of drums, a dazzling blaze of light exploded over their heads. Clara saw a figure in silver spangles floating down like a fairy on a swing. The bear had gone. The acrobat started to perform, balancing on a narrow pole above the ring. Her body twisted like slow stretchy elastic, losing itself in knots then flipping free in a brilliant chain of backward somersaults. A roar rose from the darkness.

'The bear was like a human being, this woman is more of an animal than the bear!' her father shouted, laughing.

Clara felt a mysterious wave of excitement tingle through her from the unknown man beside her. Her father.

The six pallbearers advanced slowly in perfect rhythm, Clara in the middle, bearing the once mythical stepmother whose long shadow had darkened her childhood.

A blur of traffic filtered into the pokey lobby. Outside the air was luminous, another perfect summer's day awaited Clara, in Paris in the late seventies.

'It's Friday, Clara.' Monsieur Roger's voice trapped her as she slipped past the foot of the stairs, heading for the door. 'You're behind with your room.'

Clara's stomach turned over.

'You'll have it Monday, I promise,' she assured him lightly. 'I'm still waiting to be paid for a job, I don't know what's going on with them . . . Film people!'

'That's what you said last time. You're four weeks late now,' his eyes hardened and bored into hers, 'The tourists will be arriving soon, I can't keep your room indefinitely.'

He averted his gaze with a flicker and pretended to read through the bookings in the open ledger. Garish posters for the Crazy Horse and the Alcazar hung in the cubbyhole behind the reception desk.

'Monday morning. Cash. OK?'

Clara gave him a dazzling smile and sashayed out, his eyes creeping up the back of her legs like worms, out into the dappled sunlight on the Boulevard Saint Germain.

Her heart was pounding, her mouth felt dry. The instant rush of adrenaline had left her panicky. How much longer could she go on like this? Something had to change. She'd be twenty-eight in August. Too old to be living on the edge.

A figure walking past waved and she jumped. It was Jean-

Jacques, Robert's assistant director. She waved back as he dived into the Brasserie Lipp two doors down. She'd met him on the shoot, although he'd been friendly and helpful she was soon aware he didn't like her. He was Corsican, like Robert's wife.

She'd seen Robert two days ago, he was off to Palombaggia that evening with his family. It looked the most beautiful place imaginable, straight out of an ancient Greek myth. 'We'll go there,' he said, tickling the nape of her neck, 'You'll love it.' Then he jumped out of her narrow bed and started dressing. 'Hey, come back . . . ' she held out her arms to him and he changed his mind. Pulled off his jeans, slid between the sheets on top of her.

She'd played a tightrope walker in his film, that was how she met him. As she took her place before the camera the blaze of light welcomed her and her whole being sprang to life. Poised on a tightrope three feet above the floor (they were using a stunt girl for the high shots), she felt Robert's eyes on her like a hawk. The silence intensified. She slid a foot forward, then sensing the warmth of his approval she opened up like a flower.

It was a small part but it could be her breakthrough. She had to hang on until the film came out. The last deal with the distributors had collapsed two weeks ago.

'Fucking assholes!' he raged in her tiny room, 'They want to change the end and cut the scene with the cheetahs. Fuck them!'

He was sheer happiness, he was torture. Having sex with him swept everything else away. The pressure of his lithe body and his brown eyes laughing into hers felt like coming home. With Robert life was rich and extraordinary, the future a glowing promise.

In the gaps when he vanished into his shuttered-off marriage darkness took over. Despite her resolutions to be independent and enjoy her freedom, insecurity and loneliness crept up on her.

If she could leave the hotel she'd be free. Free from the wild rush of pleasure when they ran into each other. Free from the sexual proximity of Saint Germain.

She stood on the wide dusty pavement. Life flowed all around her. Ethereal blonde models swinging glossy carrier bags chattered in front of shop windows. Street vendors sold *Le Monde*. Couples flirted over drinks on café terraces while the steady stream of traffic braked at the lights on the corner of the rue de Rennes. A successful long-haired musician crossed the road with a long-haired Afghan hound, talking to a record producer Clara recognised from meeting briefly at a party.

She drank a coffee at the bar of the Tabac opposite. A brandy would be better. But no one was inviting her.

She paid for a handful of tokens and forced herself into the phone booth.

'He's away, dear. His pupils are on holiday, he'll start life drawing classes again in September. If it's about modelling call back then.'

Clara hung up with a shrug. The peanuts the aging Argentinian painter paid her for posing naked in the chilly studio wouldn't come near to paying her hotel bill. She steeled herself and tried the casting director for the musical comedy. He took her call but he'd obviously forgotten who she was: 'That English accent is cute, sweetie, but you'll never play Molière!'

Norman was back in town, his rich banker still in the frame. Much as he adored Clara, he couldn't risk blowing it by tap dancing with her in the metro.

She toyed with the idea of calling her sister but their last conversation rankled. 'Get real, Clara! Tony's lost his job and our library department could go next. While you're swanning around Paris we're struggling to survive in Thatcher's England!' Sandra relented slightly, 'Look, if you're in trouble, come back to Birmingham. We can put you up on the sofa until you find your feet.'

Clara inserted the last two bronze-tinted tokens into the slot. What would Sandra say if she knew she was calling their father? Breaking the unwritten law bonding the two sisters since childhood, engraved in flesh by their mother before she died: Never ask him for anything.

We don't need him. We're doing fine.

Their father played by the rules too. The rare times they met he admired Clara's exotic Parisian life and the promise of her brilliant acting career, taking care to mention how hard up he was with two young children to raise, the organic pig farm to run single-handed with Eliza, family health care.

She listened to the phone ringing. This was it. She was going to come clean. Ask him for help . . .

'Hello?'

Damn. It was Eliza, not her father.

'Eliza? Hello, this is Clara. I'm calling from Paris . . . ' Silence. 'Er . . . How's dad?'

'We're in good order. Not getting any younger.'

Clara laughed dutifully. She gulped, ready to ask to speak to him . . .

'What can I do for you?' A voice like dry ice.

Clara hung up.

She drank a brandy standing at the bar, then a second one. Stepping out onto the boulevard the sunlight hit her and she staggered, she hadn't eaten since breakfast. She remembered she had a bar of chocolate in her room.

The make-up artist on the film had told her about the Hotel Taranne. 'It's right on the Boulevard Saint Germain, next to Lipp. But up on the sixth floor they have four tiny maid's rooms at thirty francs a night. With breakfast. I know Monsieur Roger, I'll introduce you.'

The room reminded her of a Van Gogh painting. The narrow bed stood alongside one wall with the bedhead fitting into the corner next to the window. If she sat on the edge of the mattress she could write at the small rickety table against the other wall.

There was a wooden chair with three rungs and a straw seat. A tiny white washbasin. All her possessions – a jumble of clothes and shoes, a few books – were in the wardrobe along the far wall with her two suitcases perched on top. The sun shone in the high window every morning and painted the little room yellow. Like Van Gogh's room in Arles.

In the beginning she still had money from the film. She lived a charmed life, dancing in and out, light-hearted with hope. The quartier was her playground, the hotel her home. She was a favourite with Monsieur Roger and his staff of three. When she woke up she'd ring reception and he'd put her breakfast, hot coffee and a tartine, in the lift and send it up to the fifth floor. Then she'd run down one flight of stairs barefoot in a t-shirt and carry the tray up to her room.

Suddenly, passing a shop window, she caught sight of a tall, long-legged silhouette on tottering high heels. She stared back blindly at her reflection, the mass of wavy red hair tumbling onto her shoulders, her emerald green satin jacket. A shooting pain stabbed the inside of her mouth and she flinched. She probed the danger zone cautiously with her tongue. The tooth wobbled. She felt sick.

Eventually she noticed the man in a grey suit watching her. He was short and nondescript with sparse mousy hair. She caught his eye in the shop window and looked away quickly. He pulled a brown leather wallet from inside his jacket and flipped it open. A row of crisp bank notes, meticulously aligned with a millimetre between each clean-cut edge, drew her gaze like a magnet. She shook her head haughtily but he thrust the wallet closer, his pleading eyes locking with hers. Clara shuddered. Yet she couldn't walk away, she was hypnotised by the banknotes overlapping like smooth coloured ribbons. He waited, imploring and arrogant, for her to take a step over the edge . . .

Clara's foot slipped. She lost her balance and grabbed the nearest granddaughter, the lightweight coffin escaping from her fingertips. The girl wobbled on her high heels and went flying, banging her knee on the floor. As the coffin shot forward Neil leapt to the rescue but only managed to launch it out further. The man behind swore under his breath. Like a film in slow motion Clara watched her stepmother's coffin topple sideways and fall. An incredulous giggle that she couldn't repress bubbled up inside her chest. A cardboard box of bones . . .

Her joyful peal of laughter from the chapel took Sean by surprise. He bet it was the tall one with the red hair, she'd caught his eye on the steps with the family group. He straightened up from pruning his favourite yellow Pilgrim rose. During the eleven years he'd been gardening here, in the Haven of Remembrance, he'd never heard anyone laugh. He found himself grinning as he listened to the blithe cascade of her laughter. He felt young again. Young and free.

SITHY HEDGES

White Buttons

Fred drove into the large car park, directed by uniformed traffic police. He was confused. It seemed that just a moment ago he had been driving to the large electronics superstore, the one that he treated like his second home. But somehow, this was not the one. Had he taken a wrong turning while his mind was on autopilot? The whole scene before him looked very odd. The huge warehouse before him was grey and imposing. There were many cars, people and a hideous number of officials directing the cars into slots. All the cars were grey, different shades of grey. He sat astonished, staring at his bonnet, which was also a dark grey. Fred knew his car was red and had been for the last four years. He must be dreaming.

A knock on his window halted his thoughts and a calm official urged him to move forward while another pointed to an empty space. He decided that he no longer wanted to try out this superstore and attempted to wave frantically at the official indicating that he was turning back. The official smiled and stood with his arms folded watching Fred patiently. Fred could not reverse. No matter what he did the car would only move forward and towards the allocated parking space. He banged his fists on the steering wheel, 'What the hell is going on!'

He sat furious while the officials had now moved on to direct other customers. People were walking towards the grey building. They were all dressed in grey to match their cars. Fred could see that his shirt and trousers matched his car, a very dark grey. He was panicking and wanted to punch all the officials. He had always been in control.

'Would you like some help, Fred?'

'How the hell do you know my name? Who the hell are you? What's going on?'

'I guess you're not a believer. It always throws them!'

'What the hell are you talking about? Believe what?'

'To put it bluntly, you're dead, Fred. Fred is dead. You're here to be processed'.

Fred burst out laughing. He stepped out of the car and bent over and doubled up with exaggerated guffawing.

'I am very much alive, and this is a dream or maybe a nightmare!' Fred shook his head in disbelief.

'Would you like me to pinch you, Fred, to see if you wake up?'

'Funny guy! I suppose you're angel Gabriel's second cousin removed or something!'

'I'm not an angel yet, I've still got a lot of white buttons to collect.'

'I give up. I'll just go in the store and look for a new TV for my media room as planned. It's all too crazy, I'm just going to ignore the peculiar and carry on as if nothing is wrong. And where the hell is Georgina!'

Georgina, his wife, was getting deaf, slow and irritated him constantly. The only way to keep her in check was to berate her with the occasional slap. And now she had disappeared! How dare she leave the car without his permission.

Fred marched towards the entrance where more people were jostling to get in. There must be a sale or special offer, as he had never witnessed such a crowd.

Inside, there were no shelves, aisles or products of any kind, only long queues. It felt like the customs or immigration section at an airport. There were too many people for him to turn back and he found himself stuck in a queue like all the others.

The words that the official had said came back to him, 'Fred is dead'.

He placed his hand on his forehead trying to recall everything before he had ended up at this strange store.

He had woken up at his usual time of nine o'clock. After his shower, he had put on his white T-shirt and jeans. Breakfast of fried eggs on toast and a pot of tea had been laid on the table by his wife, who was busy clearing up in the kitchen. He had then left the house, ordering Georgina to get in the car.

His drive had been slowed down by a trail of sponsored cyclists all of whom he had hooted to get them out of the way. They frustrated him on a Sunday morning, and he would have happily mowed them all down if it had been allowed. He remembered the mini roundabout; he knew where he was going and never bothered to indicate as it seemed to him that it was nobody else's business anyway. That was the last thing he could remember before he had found himself in this ridiculous situation. So, either this was a dream or the whole morning had been a dream. It was suddenly his turn.

'Fred Masters, how many white buttons have you got?'

'What the hell are you talking about? I have no white buttons!'

Fred saw other customers produce pouches and spill out

small white buttons onto the counter. He suddenly felt quite worried. Why did he not have any white buttons even if it was just a dream.

The official raised his arm and immediately two guards dressed in black with red trim appeared.

'Sorry, Fred. You will have to start at the bottom'.

'What? Where can I get these white buttons? Nobody told me about these. How much do they cost? I can always find a way to pay for as many as I need!'

'They are not for sale. They have to be earned'.

'So, what do I need to do?'

'Just be nice!'

'You fucking idiot! Nice does not get you anywhere! I work hard and work smart! You know nothing!'

Magically, he spotted Georgina at another queue, wearing a light grey silken dress. She was pouring an array of glossy white buttons onto the counter. He leapt forward, pushing aside everyone in his way.

'Georgie! Georgie! Where the hell have you been? And give me those buttons at once, I'll take charge!'

'Oh, hello Fred. You're welcome to all of the buttons, but I don't think they will allow it.'

Fred reached out to snatch the pouch and sweep up the buttons, but his hands simply could not grasp them. No matter how hard he tried, he couldn't even pick up a single one with a delicate touch, it was as if his hands passed through air.

Fred found himself being gently taken away, unable to exercise any resistance.

'All this nonsense has gone on for long enough! Where the hell are you taking me?' he shouted as they entered a lift.

'We're going down, Fred.'

'I want to get some bloody white buttons! Do I have to be a fucking good boy or something equally cretinous?!'

'That's right be a good boy and you will get a white button. If you collect enough you will start to work your way up.'

Fred calmed down, hoping and praying that this was a dream and he wasn't going down to Hell in a lift simply because he did not have any white buttons. It made him angry that Georgina had a huge supply, when she had done nothing to deserve it.

A sudden wave of realization passed through him and made him shudder. It lasted just a second. A flashback of how his parents had always made him feel unworthy. They had not even come to his wedding. He had resented his marriage ever since, but Georgina had stayed dutifully at his side. A lonely tear leaked from his eye and as he brushed it away, he gasped to see a pearly white button appear in his palm.

WENDY OBERMAN

The Glove Maker

It is the day of my betrothal in the year 1675. I wake at sunrise. I cannot actually see the rising sun. There are no windows in my small sleeping area in our two rooms in the heart of the Jewish Ghetto in Venice. It doesn't matter to me that I can't look out. In my imagination I can see the light of the day kissing the stones, casting them into gold, changing the water of the canals from the inky black of night to rich green. How beautiful it must be, as, beyond the walls of the ghetto Venice wakes to its day.

I can hear the shouting of the guards as the gates that both imprison and protect us are heaved open for the day. Inside the Ghetto itself, the spice merchants, the silk dealers, the money lenders, are opening their places of business. All Venice will come to Ghetto to do trade, to arrange loans, to discuss matters of law, to talk of poetry and music – even to gossip. It is a golden age for us Jews here in Venice. We are safe in our Ghetto, as long as we are useful to the Venetians. Yet we are not free to come and go as we wish. It is only our doctors who are able to travel the canals at any time of day or night to treat their patients. They do not even have to wear their distinguishing yellow caps on their heads or have the yellow circles upon their chests. But for the rest of us, only able to leave the ghetto between sunrise and sunset, yellow is the colour that marks us as Jews. But we are grateful. We are not, currently, killed in the streets as we are in every other place. The Council of 10 who rule Venice protects us for as long as it pleases them.

My world is very small. I am controlled by my father, by the rituals of my faith, and by the rules of an outside world that excludes me. I will try not to think of any of that today.

My father has chosen my husband. I have never met him. I know he is 17 years of age, and he hails from Leiden. I am 14 years. My birthday was three weeks ago. I will meet my future husband this afternoon at our betrothal party when he will tell my father that he has come to my father's house to take me for his wife. I will be his wife from this day and forever. My father tells me that love will come. I choose to believe him. I love my father. I trust him with all my heart. My father is a learned man. He is a spice trader, and fortune or God has smiled on him. We live in the New Ghetto, a better part of our confined area, in our rooms at the very top of a tall building. It is the tallest in Venice. We have a servant, Esther, who has cared for me all my life. My mother died when I was born. My father never married again. He said to have known love once is enough and he had his child. Of course, the women of our community tried to match him with a widowed soul, someone suitable, someone with an inheritance to bring with her, but whatever our circumstances, and they were difficult sometimes, my father said that we were better alone together than with some outsider trying to tell us how to live our lives.

As I have told you, father is a learned man, a Rabbi. Many people from the outside world come to ask his opinion. He is respected. Once, the King of England, Henry VIII, sent an emissary to ask for my father's interpretation of a chapter from Leviticus 18.16 which prohibits marriage to a dead brother's widow. It seemed that this King wanted to dispose of his older wife who had been married to his brother and take for himself a new bride. My father told me that the blood of desire can make men mad. And that certainly this King was mad. He composed his answer carefully, one must always be so careful when one is a Jew. Offence or discourtesy can mean banishment, or even death. Not just for oneself, but for our whole community.

My father supports us through his trade as a spice merchant and arranging loans for the rich Venetians. But now it is no longer to be just us. The match had been decided. My husband from Leiden will come and live with us, he will work with my father, he will study with my father, and he will love my father's daughter. At sunset I will be dressed in my finest clothes with a baroque pearl at my throat and pearls around my neck. I am but an offering. I try not to mind.

Today, my father has permitted me to go over the Rialto Bridge. I will go down a small alley, so narrow that only one person at a time can tread the cobbles. Half way down the alley, I will descend a small step and I will enter the shop of the Glove Maker. I am to have a beautiful pair of gloves, gloves that my father will give me as a gift for my betrothal.

I am excited. I want my gloves to be made of red satin embellished with black lace. When I am finally a married lady I will wear my beautiful gloves to the synagogue. Esther has said it is not seemly for a young bride to wear red, but my father has rebuked her and told her I am to have whatever I want.

I make ready for my day and then I tiptoe into my father's

cabinet. He returns from the synagogue after morning prayers. He always takes a coffee with a biscuit made of almonds. This is the time he works on his accounts. No one is allowed to disturb him, except, of course, for me. I creep towards him, I am silent. As a small child I was sure he could not see me. It is a game we still play. He acts as if he does not know I am there, and whilst he is concentrating, I devour the rest of his biscuit. It is then that he will notice me. He always pretends to be angry, but of course, he is not angry. I am his only child, but I am to be married. I know I will no longer be able to play our game.

On this special morning my father asks me, 'are you going to the Glove Maker?'

'Yes', I reply.

'Choose well my daughter. Choose what will make you feel like a queen. For soon you will be a queen. No longer a princess.'

'Will I love him?' I ask my father again.

'Love will come' my father says again.

I go with Esther to the Glove Maker. The Glove Maker tell us that his Apprentice will make my gloves, but he will oversee every stitch.

I choose the fabric, a magnificent red satin, and the thick black lace that looks as if it were a web that had been spun by a spider. Esther clicks her tongue with disquiet. I ignore her. Now is the time to make the pattern.

The Glove Maker calls for his Apprentice to came into the work space. The Apprentice carries with him the roll of red satin.

I look up at him as he stands in front of me, holding the rich red fabric, and I know, like a bolt of fire, that I have met love. Love has come to find me, in the eyes of a Gentile, in the eyes of a stranger. His hair is blonde, his eyes are green, his face gentle. I can see the shock in his eyes and I know love has met him too.

He takes my hand, his fingers shake. I enjoy the feel of his skin on mine. Is this love? How can it be? I did not know him. I have not even heard his voice.

'I am told you want red satin, with black lace,' he says.

His voice is quiet, he lifts the ends of his words, like the trill of a harpsichord. I have never known a voice like that.

'Yes,' I say.

'Your father spoils you', the Glove Maker says. 'Red satin will stain. You should have black gloves, so much more practical.'

'Tush,' interjects Esther, 'neither red or black are suitable for a young bride!'

We do not hear the Glove Maker nor Esther. Neither I nor the Apprentice.

'The red satin will look beautiful,' the Apprentice says.

'I know.' I reply.

His movements are stronger now. He lifts my hand with authority and lays my fingers down on the fabric. He takes a knife and cuts through the fabric with such a skill and at such a speed. I love the movements his hands make. I watch as the blade comes close to my fingers. I want it to come closer still, to actually feel the steel against my skin.

'Be careful of her.' Our servant Esther snaps.

'I will be very careful of her.' The Apprentice replies to Esther. He looks at me.

'She is to be betrothed tonight,' Esther tells the Glove Maker.

'Betrothed?' The Apprentice whispers his question.

'Yes.' I whisper back.

The Glove Maker speaks, and says, 'he will stitch the gloves and deliver them to the Ghetto.'

My heart drops. Will I never see the Apprentice again?

'I can collect them', I say boldly, not wondering how I would slip out of the ghetto, how I would meet him, but knowing I have to see him. My heart shivers. I cannot bear it if I never see him again.

The Apprentice says nothing, but his eyes hold mine as he

wraps the satin around the skin of my arms. His fingers linger, caressing as he smooths and tightens the material over my arms. I close my fingers tightly, feeling the wisps of pleasure. He is looking at me so intently.

'I think I should see you put on the gloves.' He speaks so quietly. 'I want to see you put on the gloves.'

I nod. I cannot speak.

The Glove Maker is distracted. A beautiful lady, her hair coiled on her head makes her entrance. The heels of her shoes are so fashionably high that she totters rather than walks, needing her servant to support her. She looks at me, but then seeing the yellow head covering I am forced to wear, the head covering which proclaims me a Jew, dismisses me as if I am not there. She engages the Glove Maker in conversation, dithering over a turquoise lace embellished with red ribbons, gold lace and white pearls that I think vulgar. She would look wonderful in grey silk.

'If you stay whilst I stitch the gloves,' the Apprentice says, 'I could fit them around your fingers. I will sew them, and they will fit you better than any other glove that has been made.'

'And the Glove Maker?' I ask.

'He will take his lunch. He will not return till three. But what of your servant?'

'Esther' I clear my throat, I try to be assertive, 'please go to the market and buy some spinach, they must be young leaves, and some sultanas, and onions. I will make spinach stewed with sultanas for the feast tonight.'

'You will make it?' Esther says, her voice escalating with each word, there is nothing musical about her words, it is with incredulity and anger.

'I am to be a bride. I will make my betrothed a dish.'

'We have sultanas, and onions, and the spinach we will get on our way back,' Esther moans. 'I am tired. I need to rest.'

'I will make a space for you, as soon as the Glove Maker is

gone,' the Apprentice says, 'and I will offer you a little wine for you to drink.'

Placated, Esther turns her watery eye on the Apprentice and smiles at him. He tightens his grip on my fingers. I tighten my fingers in his grasp. I see the flare in his eyes. He feels it too, the delight.

The Glove Maker knows my father, he sees no harm in leaving the Apprentice with me. After all I am accompanied by my servant. As soon as The Glove Maker leaves, the Apprentice makes a place for Esther to sit. He pours her a generous glass from a flagon of wine. We watch while she drinks, and then slowly, almost slyly for fear anyone is aware, her eyes flicker and then shut. Her head goes back, her mouth opens. She begins to snore.

The Apprentice laughs. He gets his needle and his thread, and he stitches, quickly, so quickly around my arm, around my fingers, until the glove is taut. He cuts out the lace and lays it on the glove, stretching it over the red fabric, covering each of my red satin fingers, even my thumb, taking his time over my thumb. I shiver. I love him.

'I will have to complete them without you. I need to complete the stitching on the inside of the gloves. I will bring them to the Ghetto. Promise me that whenever you put on your gloves, you will think of me.'

'I will.' I look at him, into his eyes, seeing darts of yellow in the jade green of his irises. I want to touch his face with my red satin gloves. I see the way his lashes curl.

'I wish I could dance with you.' I say the words before I know I am thinking them.

He stands up and puts his hand around my waist, and draws me to him, guides me with silent steps, small steps.

'I wish I could be the first' he says.

I shiver.

And then he bends his head towards me and brushes my

lips with a kiss.

I want to kiss back.

I cannot.

We stand apart. Awkward, suddenly strangers, after such an intimacy.

I look away.

'May I remove your gloves?' he says.

I hold out my hand. And then it comes again, the surge of delight as gently and skilfully he unpeels my arm from the red satin and black lace covering.

Esther stirs. Esther wakes.

The Apprentice removes the other glove.

My arms bare, I am ungainly. I want to cry. I feel the tears prick my eyelids.

'What time will you deliver the gloves?' Esther asks the Apprentice.

'It will be before sunset, before the gates of the ghetto close.'

'Before the betrothal,' I whisper.

Did Esther glance at me. I do not care. My heart is breaking. I will never see him again.

'Yes.' He replies to her. He does not look at me again.

We leave the Glove Maker and return to the Ghetto.

'What about the spinach?' Esther says sharply.

'I don't want to do it now. The glove making tired me.' I say. I know I sound petulant.

I go straight to my bed in my alcove.

I dream of him. Of the red gloves. I long to be with him, to watch him cut and stitch. I wonder about him? Does he have a betrothed? I am jealous of a nameless person who would cook and wash for him. I cry in my dream.

I awake at dusk. I can hear the gates closing. I run into the sitting area. There on a cushion are the red gloves. With them is a red rose.

'Apparently from the Glove Maker. For your betrothal.' Esther says tartly.

'How kind' my father said innocently, 'a rose for my daughter.'

I feet a surge of shame. The Apprentice has sent the rose. Love has come. Love has kissed me. My joy flushes my cheeks.

'The Glove Maker came himself,' my father said. 'We took a drink together. Two fathers grieving for the loss of their children. The Jew and the Gentile.'

I look at my father.

'The Apprentice is the Glove Maker's son. He is betrothed too. He will go to Florence, to marry the daughter of a master of the trade. We let our children go to a new life so we can grow old without fear for them,' my father tells me.

'I will never leave you.' I tell my father. 'And the Apprentice will never leave his father. Not in our hearts.'

My father hugs me. I hug him back, but even as I do, I know I am no longer his little girl. He knows that too.

I dress for the betrothal. And right at the very last moment, before I am to be presented, I put on my red satin gloves trimmed with their black lace and I remember the touch of The Apprentice.

Awaiting me in the synagogue is the dark-haired suitor, my betrothed. I walk towards him, I do not falter. I do not need to falter, I feel the Apprentice's fingers in every ripple of satin cloaking my arms, supporting me.

OLIVER RUGEN

An Obligation to Endure: or How Small Things Matter

I

'A little flat in Kennington – that sounds like a title to a short story don't you think?'

Robert grunted intending assent to halt the conversation. Hardly, he thought, considering that is where he lived often feeling trapped in a story that couldn't be told any other way. Writing, as a form of self-expression it seemed to him, was somehow wrong. Beyond the excitement of capturing thoughts – it just gave order to experience which might otherwise have been felt differently, more acutely, more real and even more truthfully. Thinking a thought, speaking a thought and writing a thought, each can carry the moment, each is different, but the act of writing contains an obligation, the legislative power of the written to control, tame, pin down and channel – perhaps expressing a need to order and leave a mark in fluid space? As Wittengstein once remarked in conversation: 'And if there were only the moon there would be no reading and writing'. But, what choice did Robert have? Pen in hand, he would have to crawl through the meaning between the lines as under a gate, and trust the place it led to.

Leon's observation, delivered with an air of self–amusement, entirely neglected the weight of Robert's experience – but he indulged Leon, knowing no amount of words could convey the reality of his life's precariousness. Was it character, personality, material status, or something along the way, that limited some in their compassion for others? To be alive, it seemed to Robert, is to live on the edge of sharp experience, embodied beings that we are. Taking nothing for granted was just a way of life to him. And to feel life intensely was possibly itself a gift. But Robert knew all this meant little to Leon who nevertheless had cultivated a predilection for music, architecture, fine wines, art and wealth. Another self-made man who had caught the surf which surged through 1980s Britain for those looking for the ride up.

And there lay Robert's central difficulty. How to communicate? He knew in the end all he had was the power of persuasion, and so writing came by default.

II

Is by default the same as by accident? Anyhow, that is how Robert ended up renting at the top of this narrow Edwardian house, just big enough in its day to house a live-in domestic; part of a terrace in a maze of narrow streets behind a major junction nestled in the Thames' curve giving easy reach to six crossings. The main room looked down on open space, bomb damage from the doodlebugs of the second world war; now a car park fringed by sycamore trees where starlings used to gather every September in large numbers decorating the air with friendly sound. Leon had stood on the tiny balcony and looked out taking in the tops of plane trees from a distant park, the tall 1960s buildings which left enough space interestingly to glimpse trains passing between midway up, and in the distance, the dome of St. Paul's comfortingly sat squat in view. He didn't comment. No doubt, Robert thought, comparing the arrangement with his Hampstead home.

For Robert, home had become as much a state of mind as anything else. But central London conveyed a charge – one time sitting at home, a sudden and unexpected flurry of snow had peppered the air and induced a sense of quietude; so too strangely had a police siren fading into the distance late one Christmas night when in bed. Both times he had felt grateful and safe. But home always depended for him on his fickle inner life. A symbol, like home, has to participate in the thing it represents to be a symbol, and so the less he felt embraced, the less support it afforded him. The little flat in Kennington was hemmed in by too many other lives whose existence seeped through the walls.

At least Robert had shown Leon a London he barely knew.

They had met some years before. Leon, it turned out, was going places in investment banking – having travelled a long way from his childhood in a remote Italian village. Education had been the channel for his ambition. He appeared to like Robert for his mind and Robert, as anyone would, responded – not from flattery, more from a sense of returning a favour. Though it never occurred to him that what they had in common might stretch to breaking point but – despite warm feelings of friendship – it did.

Leon had suggested Robert accompany him and Ingrid, his wife, on a short holiday that included brief business for him in Austria. Robert had flown with Leon's wife, who he might have found interesting, but to his disappointment only encountered the heavy side of a kind of German seriousness. She pedalled art for a Munich Art House and was intending herself to visit the Venice Biennale. Robert's mischievous suggestion that the whole fling was just expensive toys for an inflated art market was taken as a presumed attack. He didn't pursue this line, and spent the rest of the journey nodding solicitously.

The first night involved attending an opera in Salzburg at which Leon had to ingratiate himself with clients. Robert thought he hid his boredom well, but was uncomfortable with the hotel where he stayed feeling he had gone back fifty years through some Volk inspired gestalt. He let it pass. But the visit to Berchtesgaden, which he had insisted on, prompted greater prescience – the bunker passages where the Nazi elite had stowed their stolen art now, curiously, guarded by snarling dogs on chains; and the Lederhosen dressed guests in a nearby hotel – all surprising, pointed to an old menace which remained in the air.

Returning to the village where Leon and Ingrid had grown up together, a kind of tension grew between the three of them – no discernable reason, and something which, had it been articulated, could have doubtless been accommodated. But nothing was said – taking the natural course of events doesn't always lead to harmony.

After a full meal with Leon's parents, Robert became unsure of the father. He was certainly of the right age and lived on the old ghost-train route along which many had escaped from Munich to Rome on their way to their South American refuges. 'Die Schwarz,' he had said, showing the photos he had taken on a recent trip to South Africa – mostly naked women posing supplicantly for tourists. But somehow he seemed to have too many of them. Leon had mentioned a long walk in the mountains, probably the only thing Robert now looked forward to. But first there was the Biennale visit in Venice. After an early start Robert split from the other two on arrival, and nosed around the pavilions before retreating to Venice‘s passages and squares away from the crowds.

On the drive back, Leon asked him what he thought of the displays and Robert didn't hold back prompting Ingrid to stiffen with rage. Robert replied artfully that he thought some of the work showed considerable skill and imagination – but already thinking to himself that to praise these aesthetics of modernity, uncritically, was to be like people who instinctively move away from a truth that feels uncomfortable and threatening – rather than choosing to trust it – and so react defensively; ignore it; or hide in sentimentality.

He asked if they noticed a series of small paintings in the Polish Pavilion – made to look like postcards – hung across a wall like scattered jigsaw pieces; partial images of a mountain road fringed with fir trees, coiled mist blurring the road's verges, the camber taking the viewer along in a way it would be hard for any photograph to achieve. Nature returned by art to itself. This met with heads looking straight ahead and stony silence.

Robert went on . . . 'but for most of the exhibits a sense of beauty seemed submerged in shock value' – something he imagined the market could more readily exploit.

Within these moments the whole store of what aesthetics harboured and symbolised caused aspects of Ingrid's inner life to explode. She'd grown to dislike her family home in a village perched half way up a valley surrounded by steep sides –barely open to direct sunlight even in summer. And, to hear Robert pontificate about the beauty of nature at the expense of what moved the great art houses of Europe – such ignorance was apparently too much for her to bear.

Leon's driving became faster and wilder. The electric sun roof was flicked open and closed with a loud crack each time Leon and Ingrid exchanged heated remarks worried – or so Robert guessed – that he might understand what passed between them.

The next morning after breakfast Leon took Robert aside and said he was dropping him off. Robert, at each stage in the conversation, felt his way being ushered along as an uncomfortable feeling took hold in his stomach. Robert tried to arrange his own taxi to the nearest station. But Leon insisted on driving him as though the offer assuaged the discomfort he knew he was causing. Ingrid stayed back and glared with a flat uncompromising stare. So the three set out with Ingrid in the front, on a journey Robert was not quite sure to where. The mountain scenery, so beloved by Robert, started to close in. The looming shapes of mountains began to seem less magisterial and more indifferent, almost intrusive presences. It had always been a puzzlement to Robert how such expansive beauty which Hitler had sought out to write his Struggle, could inspire such dark thoughts of singular domination and destruction. But even landscape can be a function of mood. Something of their beauty evaporated indelibly with these thoughts and the strained pressure in the car.

They took all Robert's money for petrol and dropped him off three hours later at a cross roads in Rosenheim.

They never met again.

The train guard was sympathetic and Robert spent a night sleeping out in Munich wondering what had happened. The all-is-normal cordial parting – a peck on the cheek and a hand shake – the non-recognition of an unspoken code being broken and his own incredulity, at the very thought of what had just passed. Another set of imponderables to claw at the mind.

III

From the everyday, a dread can creep in unbidden or get stoked up by spontaneous reaction. Restlessness that makes intense pressure in the head or the whole body wanting to burst out, but finding itself trapped; the self gripped by a perception of hopelessness, engulfed, cut off and alone. Anticipation – as absurd as putting paint on canvas before viewing the subject – these moments of panic and anxiety are edges, kinds of halo that surround anything and can manifest as everything. When they strike, are they thoughts, emotions, sensations or just an attack? – a mental tick, learned and repeated – a psychic charge caught in temporal uncertainty, present's past tearing at our being? Sometimes, in glimpsed realisations, a sort of sense can make its presence felt – it's all relational: there could not be even meaning itself without reciprocity; and it is with these moments a kind of obligation can seem to beckon, which dulls the edge and makes holding on possible.

EDWARD COY

The Game and How to Play it Safe

Why are you here again? – all dolled up with that look in your eye that I can tell is saying I'm angry but I don't want anyone to know so I put a smile on top of it that goes with the look – it's the fashion don't you know. Our gaze forces each other's eyes down and both sets rise up again – meeting again – like anxiously reclaiming a straight and level stare, united in a desperation to hide from each other that desperation, like children trying to outsmart their reflections in mirrors.

Why are you here again? Because of the way the game is played? Because of the way extreme wealth is handed out like a game of Three-card Monte? 'It could be you . . . ' Last night someone that looks just like you was chosen. Tonight everybody around you looks like you. It could be any of us you all presume. But it's you. *You* are chosen. But on the way to claim your prize you lose your ticket. Has anyone ever been chosen twice? You wonder. You know what to do. You get all dolled up. You hide your anger by putting a smile on top of it that goes with the look – it's the fashion and if anybody peering into your eyes thinks they can see – look away, reset and stare straight back at them the same way they're staring at you.

JEFFREY GREENSLADE

Deep North

On the morning of my escape I get up before dawn and, overwhelmed by darkness, move slowly and with difficulty around my room, as if it were an unfamiliar thing. I don't want to turn on the light as it might reveal, with unwelcome clarity, the motives for my flight which I don't completely trust. Equally, I don't want any last minute reminders of what I'm leaving behind. I've made up my mind and am determined to suppress any lingering doubts before I'm well on the road. Until then, my surroundings must be treated like an invisible enemy, lurking in early morning darkness for their chance to distract me.

Nor do I allow my thoughts to run too far ahead. Like any serious escapee I've my contact on the outside and for the moment our projected rendezvous is the only future I need.

Despite myself, at the door I stop and listen. It's improbably quiet. Besides my own heartbeat, thumping noisily, the rasping of a small mechanical clock, normally inaudible, seems to fill the room with sound. Giving me my marching orders, perhaps. Or a warning to get away, while there's still time. Before the imminent sunrise can expose my flight.

Quickly, I open the door and slip through, into a glacial rush of morning air. So this is how freedom feels. I brace against its sobering chilly blast.

I make my way through several empty streets to the bus station. Already there's a menacing light in the sky, a hint of the relentless dawn, threatening my sense of seclusion and safety.

I hurry through the darkness of the station where, at the corner of my eye, I glimpse other early travellers. Mostly work-bound, I would guess, and facing a very different sort of day. Suddenly a feeling of relief, even elation surfaces from nowhere.

In the street beyond, I see the expected huge white truck, its sides tattooed with swirling patterns of mud and the fittingly large figure leaning beside it, fixing a cigarette.

This is Cliff, tarnished motorway angel, gruffly willing to lend a helping hand. Today, my getaway man and conduct to the fabled region of the Deep North.

A giant shadow in the morning darkness, he is a match for his truck, with huge shoulders stacked against disaster. Despite his enormous frame he droops somewhat, like a bear on its hind legs, trying to stand upright. As I approach he drops down and slides forward to take my bag. Without a word he pulls open the high cabin door and slings it inside.

I know better than to engage him in casual chat. Instead, I climb in quickly, showing I fully intend to co-operate.

The nicotine-laden cabin seems vast with ample seating. As I settle into my space, Cliff grabs a small spray and puffs it vaguely into the darkness. The fusion of spray and nicotine is not an improvement. I know he likes to ride with windows open so I will just have to wait.

He needs to deal with something in the back so, for a few moments, I have a chance to relax and take in my surroundings. Outside the light may be growing but here, in Cliff's bear cave of a cabin, there's still darkness. I can't see any detail but am content to wait. Revelation will come later, with daylight and the road.

For the first time this morning I feel safe. In this womb-like space I actually relish the enveloping darkness, free from those Furies who pursued me. They were right at my heels, but now the darkness, the supporting bulk of the torn leather seats, even the strange mixture of scents breathe freedom.

For some time now I've been dreaming about the North. It seems that an old fascination has resurfaced, tied, maybe, to my oppressive sense of confinement. In my dreams, I seem to be walking inland from a rocky stretch of Highland coastline. Among wind-swept grass and heather, with distant hills, and a vista of descending valleys running in several directions away from the sea. Deep in one of these, I come upon an old stone, which I'm surprised to see. It's somehow familiar, but I can't say why.

Although I'm dreaming, the stone feels solid. I run my hand over its flinty whiteness and feel the smoothness and the chill of its touch. It's a little less than my height and improbably spherical, like a ball tossed by a giant. Chance has landed it here, in this distant spot. It could be anywhere except I know, with the mysterious certainty of a dream, that it's somewhere in the North.

On waking, I feel it still beside me. And around it a deeper presence, that of the North itself, like a call from the heart of a legendary region charged with mystical power.

The Land beyond the North Wind, or beneath the Polar stars. The direction that the poet Basho took, when he burned his boats, and made a final climactic pilgrimage to the north of

Japan. All these are part of my sense of 'northernness', with an indefinable allure beyond any physical location.

It's this strange, intense experience which has spurred my escape. My librarian's job, grindingly routine, encroaching family ties and, more recently, a growing sense of emptiness and disconnection – these have gradually forced me to the edge. Determined to avoid the inevitable collapse, like Basho I've crashed out of my former life, in quest of something beyond the mundane.

Something to be found in the North. Now with the stars in favourable alignment I've the opportunity to pursue my dream. What is it about my vision which makes it seem more familiar, more substantial than my own habitual and grounded reality?

As if in answer, the driver's door creaks open and the huge bulk of Cliff heaves itself into the seat beside me. A small light flicks on and for a moment its brilliance is blinding. When its aura fades, Cliff's huge wrinkled face is beside me, grinning cheekily.

'OK, where to guv'nor?' 'The North', I reply. 'The North it is!'

There's no more to say. Both of us know there's only one route for Cliff to take, bent as he is on his weekly mission, as an independent haulier, on a well-worn passage to the north. During one period, when he had no use of his truck, he was a minicab driver and that is how we met. One day at the library, when I knew I simply must escape, I called a car and it was Cliff, improbably squeezed into a jacket and tie, who answered. He did me a few good turns – now he is going to do me an even better one.

Cliff is a traveller and I am his apprentice. What I long to do, Cliff has been doing all his life. Roads like Cliff and he likes to be on them. Even though his preference is for the long-haul, he relishes all kinds of thoroughfares, from winding country lanes to the steep curves of mountain passes.

He was taught by a tiny Australian woman who handled big trucks with ease. There his career began, on the other side of the world, crossing and recrossing vast distances which terrified some but which for him meant freedom.

'In the desert, you can remember your name.'

But this is not the desert but early morning London with the rush hour looming. After a power-up worthy of a Saturn rocket we move quickly through the urban labyrinth and are soon at full tilt on the motorway, every kilometre taking us further from London and my past.

As daylight steals into the cabin, I can finally perceive my surroundings. As I anticipated, it's not lacking in interesting flotsam. In fact, the dashboard is a veritable beach containing fossils, crystals, and battered figurines of whales and dolphins. It's a bit like a shrine, which makes Cliff, I suppose, an itinerant priest of the Road. Round his neck he wears a mineralised seahorse while his giant arms are tattooed with yet more aquatic specimens.

Now we're at speed, his mood, varying through the suburbs, has also stepped up. He starts to regale me with traveller's tales, anecdotes of the Road. I can relax and listen, carried on the good natured tide of his reminiscence. But I also know that sooner or later he's going to ask me a question so, to forestall him, I ask one of my own. Bearing in mind our departure, I ask him which he thinks more important – the beginning or the end of a journey?

'Ah, trick question! How do you know when it ends or begins?' I recall this morning's feeling of safety in his truck.

'So safety's your thing. With me, it's being on the move and when I move I lose count of time. No endings or beginnings, it's all motion. I'm a living blur, know what I mean?'

'But you feel safe, Cliff, on the road?'

'Safety doesn't come into it. I'm caught up, I'm on the go . . . Look, you know the moment (I didn't) when you reverse on a hairpin and you see your tail sticking over the edge? You just refocus and act. But it's only later when you look back you think

'Jesus! Was I really over that drop? I'm for forward motion.'

Forward is what Cliff does best. His mood is infectious so our spirits are high when around mid-morning he suddenly leans towards me and yells 'Don't look left!'

'What is it!' I cry, startled.

'Birmingham! It's OK, we'll be past it in an hour or so.'

I can't see any obvious features in the drab motorway hinterland but, a few seconds later, I catch sight of something which makes my heart leap. An immense blue sign with a simple message – 'The North'

Cliff grabs my shoulder, laughing a huge shaking laugh. 'There you are, told you so!'

But don't ask me where the North begins!'

I'll find out when I get there. But I feel I've crossed a threshold. Now I've got real, substantial mileage between myself and my past, I can start to look forward, to the imminent future.

Cliff seems to recognise my mood as, for a while, he's unusually silent, aware perhaps that deeper feelings have taken hold. The ride becomes smoother, as if he's easing his grip on the road. The decor in our cabin settles down, the flotsam on the dashboard stays where it is, no longer in perpetual motion. I'm focused on what lies ahead, in the mysterious region that has me in its grip. What can I expect, now I've answered its call? Will it prove benign – or the reverse?

At last the road winds down and we reach the last milestone of our shared journey. I'm sad to be losing my companion, my mentor on the road to freedom. I tell him so, and get a bone-crunching hug from which I'm glad to emerge unscathed. I'll need all my strength, and my bones, for the next, most testing leg of my trip. But, buoyed by our encounter, I'm facing the future with relish.

More than a month after my parting from Cliff, I'm standing on a coastline of the North. Over the preceding weeks, by my own effort and mostly alone, I've travelled by every kind of means, and garnered several novels' worth of experiences.

Most of these I've committed to paper. And as many times as I've lifted my pen, I've rediscovered the particular grace that comes from writing. The process of creation, the mystery of the filling page, are worth all the hardship of travel.

I'm living in a remote cottage, close to the sea. With help from the few inhabitants whom I've encountered, I've come slowly to familiarise myself with the area, garnering a little of its rock and mineral wisdom. I'm grateful for this unexpected grounding in the secrets of the northern landscape.

On this day, I'm gazing seaward towards the coastal islands, which remind me that the North never really ends. Beyond this Highland coastline there is more, and again I recall Cliff's scepticism about beginnings and endings.

I have in mind to explore one of the inland valleys and so, from the high point where my house stands I descend by what seems a vast, deep furrow in the rock – a furrow ploughed by giant hands.

Despite the strangeness of the scene, I'm aware that it also seems curiously familiar. With deepening anticipation, I progress to the valley's end and there it is, my stone, exactly in the shape in which it presented itself in my dream. Of the same, nearly perfect roundness and of a height which seems to match my own. For a while I simply stand and gaze, moved by the sense of something mysterious yet deeply known.

At length, I reach out and place my hand on it, finding it every bit as smooth and flinty as I recall. It looks alien but also perfectly at home, as if possessed of an enduring wisdom that has outlived many journeys and lifetimes. Calm, at last, in its presence, I also feel that I've come home, if only to the threshold of an ever-deepening mystery.

I become aware of a slight breeze. As I stand peacefully in the stone's shadow, it grows stronger, bending the trees and causing the long grasses to sway and rustle. Before long, it's blowing with the strength of a gale and the whole valley seems in motion.

I turn to head back, but not for the last time I'm moved by the paradox of the Deep North, which seems both present and ageless, grounded yet profound. It's all these and more. Again, I'm reminded of Cliff's indifference to boundaries.

I thought the stone would be the end of my journey. Now I know that it's just the beginning.

DEBORAH BOSLEY

Story

My mother never bothered. I know, I know, it's not her fault. Well, not all of it. Any arsehole could tell you it's not what happens, it's how you react to it. I reacted to her and everything since in the only way I knew how. I got out of it. I remember getting out of it in this room twenty years ago, me and Maggie skinning up and smoking out of the window so that Mum couldn't smell it. Of course she could smell it, but what was she going to say? She'd been scared of me since I was about twelve. God, we used to piss ourselves, me and Maggie. Those were the days when the gear still worked, when getting stoned meant laughing till it hurt. It used to make everything so funny, now it just makes me so anxious that my heart bangs in my chest. I wonder why it stopped working? I wish I could go back to that time, there must have been a moment when turning back would have been an option, when it would have made the difference. Knowing me, I'd have ignored it.

It's the same with booze, that just turned on me too. You give it the best years of your life and, slowly, it turns on you like a bad dog. Somewhere between promiscuous sex and blackouts I turned into a sad, wrung-out depressive who can't handle her own feelings and self-medicates to make them go away. I'm not fussy about what I use to chase them away, anything will do. Booze and spliffs were my favourites, then I discovered coke. It was the biggest kick. I could get from nought to sixty in twelve seconds. Talk? You couldn't shut me up. I was pleased to see everybody, asking them about their loved ones. Fresh out of charm school, you should have seen me. Fast forward a year and I don't want to waste time talking to no bugger unless they have a wrap stashed about their person, and I'm pretty blunt at getting them to come across. I'll nod impatiently while they make polite conversation, but about a minute and a half is my max until I just come out with it and say: 'Got any gear?'

There's got to be some law of opposites going on here. Some strange, magnetic, repelling force. You know, the way a thing is in the beginning, will, if you keep at it for long enough, end up being the opposite and, God, knows, I'm tenacious when it comes to a drug. The great circle of life, eh? Round and round in circles, never going anywhere. No, tell a lie, you do go somewhere. If you try really hard, you'll get to rock bottom. Trust me.

It's not like you can just go back and start again, because each time you're further from where you want to be. And each time you've got less fight left in you to get up and have another crack.

Regrets are pointless, but I tell you what I'd love to know. I'd love to know what I'd look like if I hadn't been on the lash for twenty years. It's a miracle I don't look older than I do. Mum's got good skin, so I must get it from her. But when I think of the millions of fags and drinks and spliffs and lines that have been walloped into this face since I was a teenager it makes you think. When people talk about addiction they go on about the corrosion of the spirit and how we suffer emotionally. I sit here thinking, yeah, yeah, yeah, why doesn't somebody just come out and say, oh and by the way, your looks get shot to shit. I tell friends, you do not get a face this dried out and raddled without serious effort. It's like anything in life, you've got to put the work in. You can really see it in the morning after a bender. You look in the mirror and it's as if you've been wrung out like a sponge, every last bit of juice and goodness just squeezed out of you. You think this looks bad, you should have seen me when I got here on Tuesday. Jesus fucking Christ, talk about a ropey old bird. I might just as well have had bender binger tattooed on my head. Rough ain't the word, I tell you.

So, do you want to know how I got here, then? How I managed to fuck it up so completely and utterly that I ended up back in my old room at my Mum's at thirty-seven years of age, potless, homeless, loveless, jobless and brainless? It started, like I said, a long time ago, but it ended on Monday. I've sworn a thousand times that I'd never do it again, but I don't think I felt total defeat until Tuesday morning. Anyway, it was a pretty average Monday morning, up at eight o'clock and having a spliff while I put my make-up on and got ready for the job which I'd still miraculously hung onto. I work in a restaurant in the West End, a huge bloody place like an aeroplane hangar with enough room to do something like 250 covers on a busy lunch. I'm the meeter and greeter, the girl that checks your booking, shows you to your table and tells you to enjoy your meal. It's a bloody mercy that I don't have to carry plates as I'm so off my face. Drunkenness and mind alteration had their uses in my job, though. Once toasted, I could make out I really was pleased to see all those mobile phone wielding people with very important jobs and good clothes, who can afford to pay through the nose for a second-rate lunch.

Everyone at work knew I was a total maniac for getting off it but, in one way or another, most of us were at it. It's one of the great illusions that keep you going; you see other people doing it, sometimes more than you, and it makes you think, I'm okay, I'm not as bad as them. Allow for the fact that most serious boozers and junkies restrict themselves to the socially like-minded. The hard core hang together. There are of course those immaculate souls who know when to stop. But your proper drunk, your paid-up addict never reaches the finishing line. It's like being in a race with no end. You get those moments of lucidity and you think, I really do need another drink and keep fostering the illusion that you will grapple with the greed until you've shown it who's boss. Well, Monday finally showed me who was boss.

Like I said, I'm stoned before I get to work at ten, check the bookings, make sure all the menus have got the specials on them, check the tables. A typical Monday morning, we're all telling our war stories from the weekend, how out of it we were, whom we slept with, who got chucked, who fell in love. It's a great trade for that, catering, you can hide a multitude of sins with a lot of jokes and stories. Roy, the floor manager, was in a good mood, because his old boyfriend whom he's been trying to evict for months, finally moved out the day before, so he ceremoniously invites a select group of the floor staff to have a glass of champagne before the first bookings show up. If I hadn't had that first drink, I'd probably have been all right, well able to wait till the shift finished at half past three till I had a drink, but it tasted so good that I went and had another. I've got a bit of an understanding with one of our barmen, Victor. He's Italian and very shy, and when he first started work, I kind of looked out for him, so he's always been good about coming across with liquor. Lots of customers, especially at lunchtime, order just a glass of champagne, so there's always an open bottle somewhere, and on Monday I had a thirst that just wouldn't quit. After four, Victor tells me maybe to take it easy, but I reassure him that I'm fine, that I'm really enjoying myself. Enjoying myself, my arse! I'm on a big old slope and I know it, but I've started and I just can't stop. I've always been a fairly diligent piss-head, you know, doing the job well between drinks, but this Monday we're busy and the more bolloxed I get the more I'm slipping on the job, and then I'm so fucked I couldn't give a shit and I've got people queuing up waiting to be shown to tables, and a sea of arms waving credit cards at me wanting to pay, but I'm on a mission and I just keep doing this straight line from the bar to the loo, the loo to the bar. The loo, of course because I've just bought a G from slippery Tony, who lunches with us every day. He's our resident dealer and trade from the waiting staff alone keeps him in Gucci suits. After one particularly big line I decide to make a heroic effort and pull it together to clear the backlog of cards and people queuing. I was whittling through them double quick and would have been fine had not that silly cow with the hair extension who works at the film editing suite in Wardour Street not made that bitchy comment. She's waved her card at me a few times and I've blanked her, then when I get to her table she says something like, 'If you're not too busy powdering your nose, I'd like to pay my bill, please.' Cheeky cow. Admittedly, I was sniffing like a bastard and there's stuff falling out of my nose, but where, I'd like to know were her manners. Normally, I'd have managed a tight-lipped smile before turning and cursing under my breath, but fuelled by champagne and cocaine, a near maniacal defiance overcame me and I found myself telling her in a sing-song voice to go blow it out of her arse. In all my scrapes with customers over the years, and there have been a few, I have never been so carelessly and happily rude. I don't know what made me do it. Maybe it was that long glossy hair extension, or the perfect, 'I don't smoke, do drugs, or drink' complexion, but something about this woman really gave me the pip. As if that wasn't horror enough, I've got bad timing working against me. A voice behind me says, 'Let me take care of that,' and Roy's perfectly manicured hand reaches onto the table and takes the waiting credit card. He shoots me that look, you know, get your arse over here so I can bollock you, so I meekly trail behind him to the cashier's desk. He's so angry he can't speak, but his look says it all. I want to mumble an apology, because Roy has been good to me and pissing him off is the last thing I want to do but I'm so mute with charlie I can't get a word out. As the credit card machine prints out the chit to be signed, he turns and says to me, 'Get your stuff and go home.'

JANET DULIN JONES

Bonnie & Clyde

'Don't tell your mother we had lunch here, she'll be jealous,' you say. I nod, understanding as we walk through the well maintained wooden and canvas stalls of Farmer's Market in the middle of Los Angeles – on Fairfax Avenue, smack on the corner of 3rd and Fairfax.

I love this place. I really can't say why, except it's because you love this place and have been bringing me here forever – sometimes just us, sometimes with mom and Phill, but it doesn't matter the weather or the company, it is a beloved ritual, only I won't understand how strong a ritual until the market is ruined by developers who will dig up the huge and easy parking lot, destroy Mordigan's Nursery, home of the most beautiful trees, flowers and tropical rain garden in California, maybe the world, and the wonderful Gilmore Field where the minor-League baseball team, The Hollywood Stars, played for decades in the13,000 seat stadium to the cheers of the bold and beautiful – real Hollywood stars of the Golden Era. You have told me of all the times you and mom and Uncle Al and Aunt Katie used to go to the games and rub shoulders with; Rita Hayworth, Frank Sinatra, Bing Crosby, Barbara Stanwyck, William Powell, Dean Martin . . .

Wonderful stars of the day who loved a good ball game – when there were no Dodgers – which I cannot fathom – a time when there were no Los Angeles Dodgers? Gone also are the fabulous and unique mom and pop shops that sold beautiful, handmade shoes and leather purses and buttons and cameras and Polynesian fragrances and lotions, businesses where you and I know the owners by name, where the staff is pretty much the same from when I was a little girl – and will stay pretty much the same until I am near middle age and the ruination takes place to make way for that glob of ugliness ridiculously called The Grove.

The 13,000 seat stadium of glamour and stars is now a big, fat, concrete bunker which houses 13,000 automobiles; history, glamour and fun bulldozed for the all mighty dollar. How lucky that neither you nor I know of the terrible fate of our beloved spot with the wonderful butchers and produce stands and food stalls with terrific taste treats; all handmade, nothing fake or 'fillered' – real FOOD; just like it was when you and mom moved to Hollywood during the post War boom . . . the golden years, when everyone dressed to go out and you could drive from L.A. to Santa Monica in ten minutes along Olympic Boulevard and stop right at the ocean and soak up all those wonderful positive ions – day or night.

Yes, we are in glorious, ignorant bliss as we go to the Langston twins – those tall jolly identical brother butchers (legends at the market) – and buy the Taylor's Pork Roll for breakfast – they slice it a wee bit thinner – just the way you and mom like it – and we venture forth to find salt mackerel for your Sunday breakfast at the fishmonger – then it's tacos and refried beans for me at the Mexican stand that fills the guacamole with nothing but lime, cilantro and fresh jalapeños, while you go for corned beef on rye at McGee's. I order a root beer float at Bennett's ice cream, where they make the ice cream right there in front of you behind a glass wall at the back of the counter. The float is a creamy dream of sugar, caramel and cream and the ice cream is so cold it gets little bits of ice that crunch in my teeth.

They have the best ice cream ever. Once you get your hot coffee in the classic Farmer's Market 'hottle'; those beautiful little Pyrex 2 cup bottle with colourful tops to keep your coffee warm and a pitcher of half-and-half; something that does not exist anywhere else in the world; Half-n-Half, the rich and creamy necessity for your coffee as we tread up the stairs to the dining rooms that look out over the Hollywood Hills.

On a clear day you can see the Hollywood Sign and today it is clear and you can see the sign and the Observatory – a place we went to a lot when I was small, and CBS television City. I am enraptured. The Carol Burnett Show shoots there and All in The Family and already – at 12 – I am in love with film and want to be in the movie business; without any idea of exactly what that entails. We talk about this while we eat our wonderful lunches, both of us relishing every bite. You tell me about the time when you and mom were at The Brown Derby having dinner and a man came up to you, a Talent Scout for Warner Brothers. You were there eating and this man came up to you and handed you his card . . .

He said, 'You have a great look. Have you ever acted?' – You were surprised and said 'No.' The man smiled and said, 'We can teach you that, call me and come in.' You did, and you ended up doing a screen test with Dana Andrews. It was to play a young veteran in a movie he was going to do. They offered you a contract and you turned it down. When you get to this part of the story,

I am mortified, 'How could you turn it down?' I nearly shriek, and you gave me your 'dad' look; 'I was worried about having a steady income, of being any good at it.' I am bereft, my dad could have been a movie star I am thinking, but then, you wouldn't be you sitting here with me having our wonderful lunch and talking, you'd be a movie star busy at a photo shoot or away on location making a movie. I'm very happy you are not a movie star.

As a way to appease my movie-mad disappointment, you surprise me with a box of four Napoleons from the French Bakery; I'm delirious with anticipation, they are perfection! Besides being a cinephile in bloom, I am a food snob – and I appreciate how superior these are to most bakery Napoleons – goopy, over-sugared, frosted messes of bad custard and soggy pastry.

No these Napoleons are exquisite; the fine powder sugar top and the very 'vanilla-y' vanilla custard – not too sweet and not goopy – with crunchy, paper-thin mille fuille. You agree and we finish off our meal sharing a pastry, saving the others for mom and Phil. It is such a nice day and we have time on our hands, so you pick up the discarded newspaper on the empty table next to us and look to see what movies are playing. I glance over the pages as well and get excited, a re-release of 'Bonnie and Clyde' at The Beverly Cinema, just down the street; I beg, no I plead, 'Please can we see it. I know it is a masterpiece, I've read the movie reviews, it won all those Oscars and I know it's for adults; there's a lot of gunfire and kissing and I just have to see it!' I take a breath . . .

You play tough on this one, 'No, Jan, you're really too young.' I counter that I'm not, I'm twelve! I launch into my best sales pitch – 'I've watched all the film noirs on late night television and on the Saturday and Sunday movie Matinees on the local stations, I can handle it!' – and you know that's true . . .

'Don't tell your mother.' I cross my heart and hope to die and there we are, ten minutes later at The Beverly Cinema, watching the opening of 'Bonnie and Clyde.' Wow, it is violent, it is beautiful, it is sexy. I'm not sure I would have used that word then, but Warren Beatty was so handsome and Faye Dunaway was exquisite.

I remembered reading in an interview in Life Magazine that Warren Beatty wasn't going to be Clyde Barrow at first it was going to be Elliot Gould or Bob Dylan, but the role went to Beatty. And Bonnie was originally going to be Warren Beatty's sister, Shirley Maclaine. Well Beatty couldn't play opposite his sister and that's how Dunaway got the role. In the article it said that Dunaway always had wrist and ankle weights on when she was at home and when she went for walks to keep her arms and legs fit and lean and long – she wanted to look great in the film. Well it sure worked for this movie, Beatty and Dunaway, I'm telling you.

You shift uncomfortably a couple of times during the movie and check on me – but I'm in pig heaven! This is it, the holy grail for a movie-geek girl like me and you have given me focus and purpose and a role model. I want to make movies like this one. I want to write movies like this though I don't even really know what that means but I have a passion and it feels good to me.

The movie ends and I break into sobs. You have to give me a Kleenex and one of the napkins from the bag housing the box of napoleons – we had to take them in because it was too hot to leave them in the car. Lucky we did, I used all the napkins blowing my nose and as I do I hear your words, 'Don't tell your mom.' And I think to myself, 'No way, Jose.' And I look over at you as you put on your sunglasses; hell you're not Father of the Year, to me, at that moment, you're Father of the Century.

Once I have recovered, you and I take a boys room and girls room break and meet up in the lobby. I give you the biggest smile, though my eyes are red rimmed and blotchy, I don't care – we ate our secret lunch at Farmer's Market and watched 'Bonnie and Clyde' and mom will never know.

I remember all of this fifty years later when there is a screening at the BFI of 'Bonnie and Clyde' in London, where I am living and working as a writer. And I can still see us leaving the theatre in cinematic bliss. We walk to your Buick Wildcat and we talk about the movie; movie buff, to movie buff.

We are happy now . . .

BIOGRAPHIES

PATRICE CHAPLIN

Patrice Chaplin is an internationally renowned playwright and author who has published 36 books, along with plays and short stories. Her most notable work includes *Albany Park*, *Siesta* – which was made into a film staring Jodi Foster and Isabella Rossellini – *Into the Darkness Laughing*, *Hidden Star*, *Night Fishing*, and *Death Trap*.

As a Bohemian in Paris during the 50s and 60s, Patrice spent time with Jean Paul Sartre and Simone de Beauvoir. Married to Charlie Chaplin's son, Michael, and living and working in Hollywood, she was grateful to meet people such as Lauren Bacall and Miles Davis, to Salvador Dali and Jean Cocteau, who gave her a starring role in one of his films.

Patrice is a director of Northern Bridge Productions, a Charitable Trust that leads workshops based in the performing arts as a new and unique way to help fight addiction. She lives in London and her latest book is to be *The Unknown Pursuit: Three Grandmothers in Search of the Grail.*

ANTHEA COURTENAY

Anthea has been writing fiction and poetry since childhood, During the sixties, while working in advertising, she regularly published short stories in women's magazines. In the late seventies and eighties her interest in alternative therapies and spiritual growth led her to become a freelance journalist for women's and health magazines. She wrote and co-wrote a series of books in the field of mind body and spirit including *Healing Now* (Dent 1991) and *Journeys Through Time* (Piatkus 2008).

STEVEN KUPFER

Steven lectures in philosophy and lives in London.

JEFF WATERS

Jeff writes straight from the heart which is unfortunate as that's a black and terrible place. He describes his style as 'writing as if no one was reading' which is particularly accurate most of the time. He has completed two volumes of comedy horror called *Strong Meat* and an homage of fourteen tales, no less, to Huxley, and several scripts for television. He likes to explore the agonising awkwardness of life through dark humour and his work has been described as 'thought-provoking inspired and deranged'. He lives in London. Where else?

DAISY FINER

Daisy is a Spa and Travel writer.

MALCOLM BRUCE

Malcolm is a composer, songwriter and performer. He works internationally as a touring and recording artist and has recorded with artists such as Little Richard, Elton John, Joe Bonamassa, and many more. He worked extensively with his late father, lifetime achievement award Grammy recipient and member of the group Cream, Jack Bruce. Malcolm is currently composing his first opera *King You's Folly*, to be premiered at Sadler's Wells. He composes songs, music for the theatre, instrumental compositions, and improvises and continues to tread an idiosyncratic path. He has been practising Transcendental Meditation since 1991 and is a vegan.

SHANTI MAYI

Her name means *peaceful or serene mother*. She is a mystic and has been offering the wisdom of the heart for nearly three decades. She is a mother, grandmother, and great grandmother. She has travelled the world for many years to set the hearts free to love first.

CHARLOTTE TRENCH

Charlotte was born in India, date unknown; raised in London with Irish connections. She moved to Paris in the eighties and has worked in the French film industry ever since.

SITHY HEDGES

Sithy's career has predominantly been in the finance sector with several years in the Inland Revenue followed by a decade spent in the private finance sector. Her first book, *Kaali*, was self published as an Amazon paperback. Her second, *Mad Mary*, is to be launched shortly.

WENDY OBERMAN

Wendy began her career in film and television working first as a Script Development Executive and then as a Producer. She has published three novels, six screenplays, and four radio plays.

OLIVER RUGEN

Oliver lives and works in London.

EDWARD COY

Edward is an artist and writer and he lives in London.

JEFFREY GREENSLADE

Greenslade lives in South London. He went to Dulwich College then studied English literature at Cambridge and York universities. After working in the family business, he travelled worldwide to sites of cultural and spiritual significance. He has an enduring interest in Arthurian legend.

DEBORAH BOSLEY

Deborah is a writer.

JANET DULIN JONES

Janet has written feature films for Sony, Paramount, Fox, Disney-Touchstone, Oprah Winfrey. She wrote the film *Map of the World* starring Sigourney Weaver and Julianne Moore. Her original TV series, *Gramercy Park,* is being produced by AMC. Her adaptation of *What if God Were the Sun* garnered actress Gena Rowlands SAG, Emmy, and Golden Globe nominations.

Lightning Source UK Ltd.
Milton Keynes UK
UKHW011802081219
354991UK00006B/242/P